The Elevator Jolted Back into Mo... ...ssing Emma Off Balance.

Kell grabbed her and steadied her.

A spark arced between them. He wanted to deny it, but there it was in spades as he touched her. Her scent was sweet and flowery, not at all like what he'd expected.

Enemy, he thought, but it was too late. He wanted to kiss her. Had wanted to since the moment he'd started staring at her lips.

Playing fast and loose with her emotions and her future didn't seem like a very sound business idea, but it was just one kiss. Surely, he could have that. A prize he'd earned by working hard to overcome his enemy.

He lowered his head slowly toward hers, waiting to see what she'd do.

* * *

For Her Son's Sake
is part of the Baby Business trilogy: One hostile takeover, two feuding families, three special babies

* * *

If y...
tell us what yo...
#h...

Dear Reader,

Thank you all for the wonderful letters and comments you've sent about Allan's *(His Instant Heir)* and Dec's *(Bound by a Child)* stories from earlier in the Baby Business series. I'm really excited that Kell's story is here. He was always going to be the hardest one to redeem because he grew up with a lot of anger and bitterness. But he was also my favorite. He had that dark, tortured past and the inability to figure out what to do now that he had his vengeance on the Chandlers and got what he thought he wanted. And he didn't disappoint me.

Emma knew there wasn't a chance in hell that Kell would keep her on in her former role of CEO in the newly merged company. As Gregory Chandler's hand-selected heir apparent, she was the embodiment of everything that Kell wanted to destroy. But what she didn't expect was the chemistry between them. I think it's safe to say it blew Kell away, too.

I hope you enjoy the final installment in my Baby Business series.

Happy reading!

Kathy

FOR HER
SON'S SAKE

—

KATHERINE GARBERA

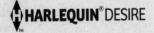

Recycling programs
for this product may
not exist in your area.

ISBN-13: 978-0-373-73344-6

For Her Son's Sake

Printed in U.S.A.

www.Harlequin.com

Books by Katherine Garbera

Harlequin Desire

Silhouette Desire

Other titles by this author
available in ebook format.

KATHERINE GARBERA

is a *USA TODAY* bestselling author of more than fifty books and has always believed in happy endings. She lives in England with her husband, children and their pampered pet, Godiva. Visit Katherine on the web at www.katherinegarbera.com, or catch up with her on Facebook and Twitter.

This book is dedicated to my parents. I always assume that everyone has a great mom and dad like I do and am surprised when I realize how special my parents are. I love you, Mom and Dad.

One

Emma Chandler forced a smile as she packed up her Louis Vuitton Neverfull bag and walked out of the boardroom with her head held high. It was bad enough to be in the lair of her longtime family rival Kell Montrose. That was stressful on its own. But to see her younger sisters paired up and happily in love with Kell's cousins, Dec and Allan, who were also Montrose heirs, was another stab to the heart.

A wave of loneliness washed over her. She should give up trying to keep herself on the board at Playtone-Infinity Games and let Kell win. Except that wasn't her style. But no matter how hard she tried to fight it, it looked as if she was on the way out of the company that she'd poured her life into for the last four years.

The hostile takeover had been a surprise, but to be

honest, she'd known for a long time that Kell Montrose intended to find a way to make Infinity Games his own and then tear it apart. It didn't matter that her grandfather—the man Kell had hated—was dead and buried or that the company had floundered a little under her guidance. She'd hoped somehow to find a heart and soul under Kell's solemn exterior. Someone she could negotiate with.

Instead she'd found a man bent on revenge, and her two sisters despite their best intentions, had fallen in love with the enemy. They had also proven themselves indispensable and secured their positions at the newly merged company. They were all finding their own place except her. She, of course, had the same chance to prove herself but she knew she was the one Chandler that Kell hated the most.

The one who'd witnessed his humiliation at the hands of her grandfather. The one Kell wasn't going to keep around any longer than he had to. The one who had exactly forty-eight hours to come up with a kick-ass idea or she wouldn't blame him for showing her the door. She thought she might have one but wasn't sure he'd give her a fair shake.

When the elevator opened, she got on and reached for the Close button. She wanted to be alone. But just as the doors started to slide shut a big masculine hand wrapped around the edge and kept them open.

She groaned inwardly as Kell stepped over the threshold and into the elevator. She hoped her forced smile would stay in place. After all, how long could it take to reach the lobby? Five minutes?

"Feeling like the Lone Ranger?" he asked.

His eyes were a silvery-pewter color that always fascinated her. They were gorgeous, she thought, but icy and intense as well.

"Not at all. Why would I?" she asked. She'd always been able to play it cool and intended to do that now.

"Your sisters have come over to the dark side. I'm going to finish bringing the last vestiges of Infinity Games under the Playtone umbrella soon."

He deserved his moment to crow, but that didn't mean she had to stand here and listen to it. She reached for the buttons again to open the doors and get off but it was too late. The elevator started moving.

"You okay?" he asked.

His face was angular, all strong jawbone and a very stubborn chin. His hair was thick and a warm, dark brown color that was almost chestnut. He wore it longer on the top and parted on the side. It was thick and curly and she almost wanted to touch those carelessly styled curls of his.

She looked up into his silvery eyes and saw a hint of humanity there. "I'm fine. I just don't like elevators. I should have taken the stairs."

"And then you could have avoided me."

"That would be a plus. I get that you hold all the cards but don't write me off yet."

"Was that what I was doing?" he asked.

He had a deep voice that she had to admit she'd always enjoyed listening to. She was a total idiot, she thought. It had been almost four years since her husband, Helio's, death and since then she hadn't been attracted to a single man. Now she was standing in an elevator way too close to one and felt a tingle of anticipation.

What the hell was wrong with her? Was this just her way of making sure she was miserable for the rest of her natural life?

"Emma?"

She realized Kell was waiting for an answer and she looked up at him and let her guard slip for just a second. "You were being an ass."

He laughed. "There's the fire I remember from the old days when we were interns together at Infinity Games. Where you were always struggling to be the best. What happened to that?"

When they were younger, her grandfather had been persuaded by the human resources department to give Kell one of the internships after his family had threatened to sue if he wasn't accepted.

"Nothing." She wasn't about to admit to a single real emotion to this man. Besides, he'd have to be an idiot not to know that losing her husband when she was pregnant hit her like a ton of bricks and then pouring her heart into this company and having him snatch it out of her hands wasn't helping.

"Nothing?"

One second away from letting him have it, she turned on him. Then she wondered why was she holding it in. It was safe to say that at this moment she had nothing left to lose. She knew it, and from the smug look on Kell's face, he knew it too.

"You really want to know what's bothering me?" she asked, taking a step forward, causing him to step back.

"I'm tired of jumping through hoops and coming up with my best ideas and then having to run down here and get them approved by you and the assembled board. I know whatever I say, it's never going to be good enough in your eyes to make up for the way you were treated by my grandfather. And I also am very aware of the fact that if I can't make this work I have no other options. All of my job experience is with a company I let get taken over."

He just stood there, his silvery eyes narrowed and his arms crossed over his chest. She knew he didn't like being called on the fact that he'd pushed her into a corner or that no matter what, he wasn't going to let her keep her job.

"What, no more comments? No more gloating?"

The elevator halted with a jerk and she reached out to brace herself again. "Better get that looked at, Montrose. I'd hate to see your empire crumble from the inside."

He stood up and pressed the button but nothing happened. They were trapped in the elevator. He hit the buttons for all the floors and then turned back to her. "Looks like we're stuck."

"Great."

She could think of other words to say but her son, Sammy, was getting to the age where he'd repeat words, so lately she'd been trying to keep it clean. But really, could this day get any worse?

At least she was alive. At least she had a roof over

her head. *Ugh*. She didn't want her mom's voice in her head. Not now. But now that it had started she was inundated with all the things she should be thankful for. Her mom had always made her list them if she complained about something.

She groaned again.

"Are you hurt? You keep making little noises," Kell said.

He looked a bit unnerved by the thought that she might be hurt. "I'm fine. I just had my mom's voice in my head."

His brow furrowed as he looked over at her.

"You know how moms are with advice and stuff. My mom's pet peeve with me was whining, so whenever I'd complain about something, she'd have me write out a gratitude list. And just now, I was thinking what a crap day this was and then I started making the list. It's a sickness, really. Was your mom like that?"

"No."

"Figures. Did she just bake cookies and spoil you? I told my mom there were ones out there who did that."

"No. Kristi Keller Montrose never did any of that. She left me with my grandfather when I was three and never looked back."

Emma stared at him for a really long time. It explained so much about Kell and made her see him as a little bit more human than she wanted to. She liked him as her enemy, pictured him as the dark, evil knight from Sammy's favorite bedtime story, but she'd just seen the first chink in the armor. Kell had clearly been the best of their group of interns and everyone had expected Gregory Chandler to offer him the managerial role in the company. But her granddad had called Kell into his office, kept him waiting and then told him that he'd never have a job at Infinity Games. No matter how many times he threatened to sue.

No, that wasn't true, she'd seen the chink a long time ago in her grandfather's office. "I'm sorry, Kell." She was sad for the boy he'd been and for the man he'd become.

"You can't miss what you never had," he admitted, as he pressed the emergency button. They were still trapped in the elevator.

Of all the things that Kell wanted to discuss with Emma, his parents weren't one of them. They'd been working together for the last six months and he had to admit, she'd been an asset to merging his company with hers. But now it was time for her to either transition into another role or leave, which was pretty much what he'd said just now at the board meeting in front of his cousins and her sisters. Everyone had looked at him as if he was the bad guy, but that was reality.

After Emma had abruptly left the meeting, they'd all been staring at him with accusation in their eyes, and he'd finally decided to just go after her. But it wouldn't change anything. And now they were trapped in the elevator, just as if they were trapped in the old feud between their families.

It had been six months since he'd initialized the hostile takeover of her family's company Infinity Games. It was now January in Southern California where they lived, and that meant chilly weather, but no snow. And he was more than happy to concede that he was very chilly toward Emma and all the Chandlers. He could even acknowledge it was a coping mechanism.

Since then, his cousins had weakened and fallen in love with the other two Chandler sisters. But Kell hadn't forgotten the way they'd struggled growing up under the bitter tutelage of their grandfather, Thomas Montrose. There had been only one thing that Grandfather Thomas had wanted and that was to see all Chandlers suffer as he had when he'd been cut out of the profits and left to see someone else developing his dreams. And the message had sunk in with Kell, the eldest grandson, who'd spent the most time with the old man. Kell's dad had been a navy SEAL killed in action and his mom had lit out for greener pastures.

"So…" Emma said after the silence stretched on, their call for help unanswered. "I guess one role you might need to fill is building maintenance."

He chuckled. "That would be a waste of your skills."

"It would, but I'm pretty sure we wouldn't be stuck in here now if I was in charge of it."

"Have you thought of anything else you can do in Playtone-Infinity Games?" he asked.

She rubbed the back of her neck and glanced over at him. He'd always thought her eyes were pretty. The color of the California sky on a late autumn day when it was clear and so blue it almost hurt to look at it.

Her long reddish-brown hair was pulled back in a chignon but a tendril had escaped to curl around her ear. He didn't want to notice it, but he did. He also couldn't tear his eyes from her lips. She had a kissable mouth, he noticed. Her lower lip was full and just looking at it whetted his appetite.

She wore a black Chanel dress with a gold accent at the neck that made hers seem long and slender. He recognized the designer because his last girlfriend had worked for Neiman Marcus and had paraded haute couture in front of him all the time.

"The only viable idea I have for a new role is to make the company's charitable arm more of a foundation. There are a few things I've been wanting to implement but there was never time in my schedule."

"Like what?" he asked. Creating a foundation would be great for the tax write-off. They were about to see some huge gains in profit from the merged company and he didn't want it all to go to taxes.

"Shouldn't I save this for the meeting in forty-eight hours that decides my fate?"

"Just run it past me," he said.

"I've been working on a prototype game at home for my tablet that would help kids with reading. I know there are other reading apps and software out there but they don't work with Sammy. So I started focusing on what he likes and working to his skills."

"That's a lot of customization," he said, but already he saw the potential in the idea. If they distributed a learning game through a foundation they could get their software into the hands of kids as they were just starting to play. So that once they were older they'd gravitate toward the Playtone-Infinity family of console and handheld games.

"Yes, but I've been talking to some of the teachers at the nursery school and they said most kids fall into four or five categories for learning so we'd create different versions based on those categories and then roll it out in test groups. What do you think?"

"I like it. I like it a lot. But you're going to need more than just one game to keep your job."

"I realize that," she said. "I've been jotting down some notes on what the charitable trust could look like and working on the job description for the chairman role."

"Fair enough. After your initial meeting with the board in forty-eight hours, why don't we have a meeting next week in your office. You can show me your prototype and your ideas for the structure of the foundation. If it's viable we'll discuss a way to make it work."

"Really?" she asked. It was almost too good to be true.

"I just said so," he said sarcastically.

"But I thought you were going to take out your revenge on the Chandlers by firing me," she said.

"Well, if you keep talking about it then I will just fire you outright. But we're family now. You and I share a nephew and an adopted niece. I've always been focused on revenge, but now that I have what I want, maybe I need to look at the future a little differently."

Her youngest sister, Cari, had a child with Kell's cousin Dec. They were engaged to be married, which meant one day soon Emma and Kell would be related. Also, her middle sister, Jessi, and Kell's other cousin,

Allan, were engaged and were guardians to their late friends' baby, Hannah.

"I'm not sure I can trust you now," she said.

"Given our family history I'd feel the exact same way. But I would have to be a total bastard to say yes to your idea and make you work hard to save your job, then not let you keep it."

"It'd be the perfect revenge," she said. "Listen, I don't want to deny that you are entitled to your position. I will work hard, but only if you are going to give me a fair chance at actually keeping my job."

"It's going to be extremely difficult to change my mind about firing you, but not impossible."

She tipped her head to the side and walked forward, putting both of her palms on his chest and leaned toward him. "That sounds like a challenge, Kell Montrose, and I am more than willing to accept it.

"We can both agree that you've made no promises and that I will have to work twice as hard to get your acceptance, but when I do, and I can guarantee that I will, you will have to keep me on not because I'm a Chandler but because you are a man of your word and we made a bargain."

Dammit it to hell and back. She was right. He was a man of his word, and now he'd have to stand behind the commitment he'd just made.

"Are you sure about this?" he asked. "There'd be no shame in walking away from Playtone-Infinity Games. I'm prepared to offer you a very generous severance package that will make you a rich woman. You'd never have to work another day in your life after this."

Her gaze met his and he saw the steely determination in her eyes. "I can't. I have a son, and Playtone-Infinity is his heritage too. What kind of example would I be setting if I just walked away."

Kell had to admit, he respected her for that. She was his enemy—that hadn't changed—but there was something about her attitude that made him want her to stay.

And to be perfectly honest it would be the coup de grace in his war against her grandfather, Gregory Chandler. True the old man was dead, but Kell couldn't help but think of how much it would piss him off to see his granddaughter bargaining with a Montrose to keep not only her job but also her pride.

The elevator jolted back into motion, tossing Emma off balance. She let her leather bag slip to the floor as she threw out her arm to try to catch herself. Kell grabbed her and steadied her.

A spark arced between them. He wanted to deny it, but there it was in spades. There was no more than a few inches of space between them. Her scent was sweet and flowery, not at all like what he'd expected.

She's the enemy, he thought, but it was too late. He wanted to kiss her. Had wanted to since the moment he'd started staring at her lips.

Playing fast and loose with her emotions and her future didn't seem like a very sound business idea, but it was just one kiss. Surely, he could have that. It was a prize he'd earned by defeating the Chandlers.

He lowered his head slowly toward hers, waiting to see what she'd do. She didn't pull back; instead, she tilted her head a little bit to the side and leaned forward in anticipation. He brushed his lips slowly over hers. They were soft. Softer than he expected. He kept the embrace gentle as he searched for some answers to the attraction he felt toward his sworn enemy.

Two

Kell didn't taste like the enemy. In fact, his kiss was exactly right, subtle and understated. He didn't take, but instead made her feel treasured as his mouth moved over hers and his hands held her steady.

She had the feeling he was as surprised by the embrace as she was, and she stopped thinking as he opened his mouth and his hot breath entered her, followed by his tongue.

She clung to his shoulders as their kiss deepened. Assertive now, he pushed her back against the wall of the elevator. His body crowded hers and she felt trapped by his presence and her own desire. His hand came up to the side of her face, the long fingers and big palm holding her as his mouth plundered hers. She shifted around in his arms. Slid her hands into his thick hair. It was just as a soft as she'd expected it to be. Ridiculously sensuous against her touch.

He caressed his way down the sides of her torso, fingers finally coming to rest and tightening on her waist, and then he lifted his head.

She opened her eyes and for the first time saw confusion and a hint of real emotion in that pewter gray gaze of his. She grabbed his tie and pulled him back, leaning up on tiptoe and taking the kiss she wanted. One that had been overdue for a long time.

He groaned as his hand tightened on her waist and he slipped his touch lower down her hips and leaned more fully into her. She felt his erection and wanted more but then the elevator pinged and the door opened. Reluctantly, she let go of his tie.

She retrieved her bag from the floor and stepped out into the carpeted hallway before realizing they weren't in the lobby. Damn. She couldn't get back into the elevator with him. Not now. She felt wild and out of control. And as she glanced over her shoulder she noticed he'd followed her out of the elevator.

She groaned.

"Making a list of things to be thankful for?" he asked.

She shook her head. Words were beyond her right now. "Where are the stairs?"

She couldn't pretend that embrace had been nothing more than curiosity. If she could…if she could, it would be perfect. But it was more than that. More than momentary lust that they'd now gotten out of their systems.

What she needed was to go back home, get back in bed and pretend this day had never happened.

"This way," he said, leading her down the hallway to one of the emergency staircases. He held open the door for her.

"You don't have to follow me down," she said.

"Hell, yes, I do. We have something to discuss," he said.

"We're having a meeting in less than forty-eight hours. We can talk then," she said.

"Really? You want to talk about how one kiss made me hotter than a horny teenager in front of our family and the board?"

She stopped and pivoted on her heel to face him. "We're not going to ever discuss that."

"Into denial now?" he asked. "I shouldn't really be surprised. That's how you lost Infinity Games."

She dropped her bag and aggressively moved back up the two stairs toward him but he simply held his ground, not at all intimidated by her anger. But she wasn't daunted either.

"You're right. I did deny we were in trouble but that was business. You are dabbling in my personal life at a time when everything is collapsing and I have no fallback point. I can't turn to my job if I take a risk on an ill-advised passionate encounter with you. And there's more than me at stake here. I have a son and I can't be a complete mess.... So believe me when I say we are not talking about that and I'm going to do my damnedest to pretend it never happened."

He tilted his head to the side and crossed his arms

over his chest. "I'm not like that. I don't forget anything."

"Well this time you're going to. Because we both know that you might give me a chance to win a role at our merged companies but privately you'd never give me anything but heartbreak. I'd have to be a complete masochist to believe anything else."

She wasn't playing around anymore. Earlier she'd realized she'd reached rock bottom, and the fact that she'd just had the most intense intimate experience in recent memory with this man made no sense to her.

"Fine. I don't think an affair is a wise idea either. For the record I'm not some kind of monster, Emma. I don't get off on hurting women."

She realized that her words had cut him and that hadn't been her intent. She shook her head. "I never thought that. I just know where you and I are concerned there is too much baggage. We're the oldest children in our families. The ones who are determined to carry on our families' complex legacy, and that makes us the worst two people in the world to ever get involved."

"I agree," he said.

"It was probably a fluke," she said. "Just the tension of the moment. I know I wanted to get the better of you at something."

He gave her a wry grin. "You haven't had the best of me."

"Haven't I?" she asked. Then smacked herself in the forehead. "I'm not flirting with you."

"I'd apologize but I'm not sorry. This doesn't have to be any more complicated then we make it."

"I agree since we're not kissing or touching again. Right?"

He put his hands up. "You fell into my arms."

"You kissed me," she said, pointing her finger at him.

"I did, but you looked up at me with your lips parted…what was I supposed to do?"

Kell prided himself on always being in control, and the fact that Emma had shaken him made him want to investigate this further. He didn't want to ignore it or let it go. He needed to explore why he was weak where she was concerned and then ensure it never happened again.

Seeing the way she was running from him made him reconsider. She had a point. He would never let himself love any woman especially not Emma. He knew that his heart was still too full of hate. He'd never really learned how to care for a woman. It didn't matter that he really didn't know her as a person, that her last name had formed his opinion of her long ago.

But his racing pulse and lingering hard-on were sending a different message. He didn't want to let her go. That's why he was standing in the stairwell debating something that he knew he should drop. It made no sense that just as he was finally reaching his life's goal, he'd find time to pursue this. To pursue her. Her?

Was he really doing this?

"I don't know. I have no idea what that was about. I haven't been attracted to anyone since Helio."

With those few words she made Kell feel something

for her. She was young, widowed and he'd recently outmaneuvered her in the corporate world. He understood that a gentleman would back away. There was no sense in chasing her.

"I'm sorry."

"Don't be. I honestly thought I'd never feel anything for a man again."

"Silver lining?" he asked, sardonically.

"In a way. I'm sorry I enticed you to kiss me," she said. "I had been a little curious about you since we were interns together."

He arched one eyebrow at her. He liked Emma when she forgot to be all buttoned up and cool. He had a feeling she wasn't going to ever be this honest with him again because it left her vulnerable. But he definitely liked seeing her this way.

"Me too. But your grandfather was always watching us back then," Kell said.

"Yes, he was. I wanted to make a good impression and you were always Johnny-on-the-spot with everything. You were a very hard act to follow."

He felt a flush of pride at what she said. When he'd been an intern he'd still had a few dreams that the world wasn't the bitter place his grandfather had always made it seem. Of course after his experience with Gregory Chandler his entire perspective had changed. It was odd to think of those days now. Kell had been a completely different man.

"What can I say? I like to be the best at everything."

"You certainly are good at kissing," she said, and

then flushed and groaned. "I'm going home now. Don't follow me."

He nodded. She was cute when she was flustered. Why was he just now seeing this? Probably because he'd taken over her company, his lethal focus on revenge had shifted somewhat.

"I won't. I'll see you at the meeting in two days," he said, pushing his hands into his pockets. He had another meeting of his own in twenty minutes; he needed to start thinking about that instead of how good she'd felt in his arms and the fact that he could still taste her on his lips.

"Thank you," she said, turning to walk down the stairs. Seeing the sway of her hips and the way the black Chanel dress clung to them made his breath catch.

"Emma?"

She paused but didn't turn, just glanced over her shoulder at him. "Yes?"

"I...I don't know if I'll be able to resist you if you fall into my arms again."

There. He'd said it. He felt better for having warned her. "I'm not saying that I want anything to develop between us. But I'm attracted to you and given how much time we spend together I wanted to be honest. If that happens again I don't know if I'll be able to stop."

She gave him a smile that was at once the sweetest expression and the saddest. He'd have to analyze it later because right now he knew he was missing something really important in it.

"Fair enough," she said.

"But then we both know that life isn't fair, don't we?" he asked.

"Yes," she said in the quietest of voices.

He realized that she'd been hurt more than he wanted to acknowledge. Part of it no doubt had come from him and his hostile takeover but more of it had come from the personal tragedies in her life. And where she was right now.

He wanted to apologize but he wasn't truly sorry for anything. If that elevator door hadn't opened, who knew how much further the embrace would have gone. He hadn't wanted it to end when it had. He was still on fire for her. But earlier she'd pointed out that he was a man of his word in business and he knew he was going to have to be the same when it came to this area too. He wasn't going to be able to just go after her like any other woman he was attracted to.

It wasn't fair to her or to him. And despite what the world had taught him, he was beginning to want life to be fair for her. She deserved it.

"See you at the board meeting," he said, turning and going back up the stairs to the executive floor. When he got there, he walked through the massive reception area. Everywhere around him were the fruits of his labor. The signs of the success that he'd made from the broken dreams of his grandfather.

Usually this walk made him proud but today it felt a little hollow. When he entered the executive corridor and saw his cousins standing around talking and smiling, he felt left out again. And realized revenge hadn't brought him what he'd thought it would.

* * *

Emma drove back to Infinity Games' old headquarters, which now served as the satellite location for the merged company. Even in the middle of the day, the drive from downtown Los Angeles to Malibu wasn't great. The traffic in this part of the world was ridiculous. By the time she got back, she was ready to call it quits but when she headed up to her office, she found her sisters waiting for her.

Clearly they were here on a mission. She suspected they wanted to help her, and that was touching but also annoying. She was the eldest. The one they turned to for advice and support. She didn't like seeing them both sitting there looking at her as if she was the fragile one.

"How did we beat you back here?" Cari asked. "You left twenty minutes before we did."

"Kell and I got stuck in the elevator together. At least I had a chance to talk to him about a new idea," she said. Then he'd kissed her and made her forget her name.

"Good," Jessi said. "He can be a dic—dictator but I think he's fair."

Fair. If she heard that word again today she was going to pick up the crystal paperweight her grandfather had given her on her twenty-fifth birthday and heave it at the wall.

"Nice," Cari said. "You usually call him other things."

"Yeah, I know, Jessie said. "But ever since Allan and I got together he said I couldn't call Kell Darth-Sucks-A-Lot anymore."

"Probably a good idea," Emma said. "Don't you two have work to do?"

"Why, yes, we do. Are you trying to get rid of us?" Jessi asked.

"Why, yes, I am. I need a few minutes to myself."

Cari came over and patted her on the back. "We're not leaving you alone until we're sure you're okay. You know you'd do the same if it were either of us in your position."

"But that's because I'm the oldest and I know best," Emma said.

"You don't. You just know three more years' worth of stuff than we do," Jessi said.

Emma had to laugh. She looked at her sisters and acknowledged how happy she was that they were both moving on with their lives. She was glad that the mess that she'd made of Infinity Games hadn't taken them down with it.

"That's so true. But I'm okay. I don't need to discuss any of this today," she said.

"Why not? I freaked out when Dec came back into my life," Cari said. "And I tried to deal with it on my own, but I finally realized I needed you and Jessi to help me out. We're stronger together, Em. We always have been."

She wanted to lean on her sisters but she had no idea what she would say to them. She had to find a way to keep her job, stay away from Kell and never again kiss him. It was complicated.

She walked passed Cari and Jessi and put her handbag in the bottom drawer of her desk before sitting down and facing them. On her desk was a picture of Sammy smiling up at her with his little toddler face. He was so sweet and precious to her. She couldn't afford to be anything other than successful in her bid to create a new role for herself at Playtone-Infinity Games.

"You don't have to worry about me," she said. "I've got a solid idea."

"What is it?"

"Taking our charity arm and turning it into a foundation with a full-time chairman."

"Great idea," Jessi said. "So that's a job for you but what will the foundation do?"

"I've been playing around with a prototype reading app with Sammy," Emma said. "It's tailored to his way of learning. I gave Kell a top-line view of what I'm thinking and he said it was worth pursuing."

"I think it is, too," Cari said. "Who's doing the coding?"

Emma had studied computer programming in college so she had a rudimentary knowledge of how to code. "I have. But it's very basic. I wanted to play with it myself and see if it would fly before I put our staff to work on it."

"I've got two guys coming off a project this week. I could allocate them to you," Cari said. As head of development it was her job to keep all their staff working.

"I don't have a budget yet. I need to put something together for the next board meeting and once I get approved I would love to have your staffing help."

"I'll get Allan to help you with the budget," Jessi said.

"Are you sure?"

"Yes, I am. If he says no, he'll answer to me," Jessi said.

Emma felt surrounded by the love of her sisters and realized that even though she'd felt alone and isolated earlier, they were here for her. They had her back and always would.

"Thank you," she said. "I'm a little too used to handling everything on my own."

"We know. It's your own fault because you made it too easy for us to just do our own thing and not really have to help you out. But this merger has been tough on all of us," Cari said.

"And if we've learned anything, it's that we need each other," Jessi added. "We got your back, big sis."

When her sisters left her office, Emma pretended that the only real concern she had was her upcoming presentation to the board. But she was lying to herself. And she knew it. She couldn't stop thinking about Kell and how his hands had felt on her body. The ache deep inside of her reminded her that she wasn't going to be able to forget that for a long time.

Three

Sammy sat off to one side of the other kids and looked down at the tablet in his hands at the childcare center on the Infinity Games campus in Malibu. It worried Emma. He wasn't antisocial, but he only engaged when he wanted to. She'd considered lecturing him on it or trying to correct his behavior but Helio's mother said he used to do the same thing when he was growing up.

There were times when Emma missed Helio so much. They'd had a whirlwind courtship and a glamorous marriage in Dubai before he'd started the Formula 1 racing season. Then he had the accident that ended his life, and it was all over. So they hadn't really ever lived together. It was moments like this when she saw him so clearly in her son that she felt the emptiness.

"Your secretary said I could find you here," Kell said, coming up next to her.

"Why are you looking for me?" she asked, blinking to clear away any lingering emotion from her eyes before turning to look at her nemesis. He hadn't lost all his hair overnight as she'd hoped. Or developed a big potbelly. Instead he was just as handsome as he'd been yesterday in the elevator. And if the way her pulse quickened was any indication, she still wanted him.

"Allan came by this morning with some financials on your new idea and I thought it might be a good time to discuss it," Kell said.

"Why did Allan bring my numbers to you? I was planning to present them tomorrow." She'd been working almost nonstop on the business plan for the foundation. Now that she didn't have to concentrate on keeping Infinity Games in the black she felt sort of free. And the foundation had been a dream of hers for a long time, one she'd never been able to talk her grandfather into pursuing.

"They're better than you expected. Allan and Dec have recommended we skip tomorrow's meeting and let you get on with the project," Kell said. "If we can go back to your office, I have some new targets I'd like to discuss with you."

That was good news. She glanced back into the nursery and noted that Sammy was watching her where she stood in the doorway. She smiled over at him and he put down the tablet and got to his feet in that awkward toddler way of his.

"I can't go back just yet," she said. "Sammy and I have a morning appointment for a snack."

"This might be why your company failed," Kell said. "You're on the clock."

"I started working at six a.m. so I think a ten minute break is acceptable."

"It might be, but business should always come first."

"That you think so might be why you're all alone," she said quietly. "It's only for ten minutes and I'm sure even the great and powerful Kell Montrose can wait that long."

The look he gave her was frosty and hard. But underneath it she could see that she'd hurt him. She had to remember what she'd learned yesterday—beneath his all-business exterior Kell was a real man. She remembered what he'd said about his mother and thought that maybe because he hadn't had a bond with her, he didn't realize how important it was.

Before he could say anything though, Sammy came over to them where they stood just inside the doorway by the coatrack.

"Mommy," he said, launching himself at her.

She scooped him up in her arms and hugged him close. Then she kissed the top of his head and set him back on the ground. He kept his tiny hand in hers.

"Hi," Sammy said, looking up at Kell.

The two had met before. Since Jessi and Cari were both moms now and engaged to Kell's cousins, their families had spent time together. And Emma actually liked both Dec and Allan. But they were nothing like

Kell. He'd always seemed out of place and uncomfortable around the new babies and around her son.

"Hiya," Kell said. "What were you doing on the tablet?"

"Playing a game."

"One of ours?"

"Mommy didn't make it," Sammy said. "It's snack time."

"I heard," Kell said. "Can I join you?"

What? She looked over at him and he raised one eyebrow at her in response.

"Yes. Mommy made enough for me to share," Sammy said.

They followed him to a table where three other children were already seated. The chairs were tiny and as the nursery teacher brought over a chair for Emma, she looked at Kell. There was no way his big frame was going to be able to perch on this tiny chair.

He just sat down cross-legged on the floor at the head of the table. Sammy sat next to him in front of his *The Avengers* lunchbox and opened it up. He took out a package of raisins and placed a few in front of Kell and then couple in front of Emma.

"Thank you," she said.

"Thanks," Kell said. "What game were you playing again?"

"Music," Sammy said.

"It's a program that teaches kids to play simple melodies. They can sing along with it and follow a little bouncing grape on the keyboard."

"What can you play?"

"Can't take it away," Sammy said, popping a raisin into his mouth. "It's Mommy's favorite."

"Is it?" Kell asked, glancing over at her.

"Yes. He means 'They Can't Take That Away From Me.' I like old jazz so he is sort of growing up listening to Ella Fitzgerald and Louis Armstrong. Plus it's a duet and we sing it at night before bedtime, don't we?"

Sammy nodded. "Uncle Dec plays me rap so that I'm not—what'd he call it?"

"Stodgy," Emma said.

"Sounds like Dec."

She could tell that Kell had more questions but Sammy started talking to the little girl, Anna, next to him. They were trying to swap snacks.

Kell turned to Emma. "I have more questions."

"I know, but he's three and it's snack time," she explained.

"After snack time then. I want to know why he likes his game," Kell said. "Do the other kids play with tablets as well? I recently read an article about kids in Estonia who are learning to program robots at the age of seven. Your idea for the reading app is right on trend."

Great. "I bet you're glad you didn't just fire me outright."

"Don't get cocky. You still have to prove you can make it work."

Of course she did.

As far as mistakes went, this was one was colossal. He'd told himself he'd come to the Malibu campus of Playtone-Infinity Games to meet with Emma about her idea. But he knew that was a lie. As soon as he'd entered the building he'd felt a zing of emotion go straight through him.

He'd thought of nothing but how she'd felt in his arms the day before. He hadn't slept or been able to concentrate on his five-year plan as he'd gone for his run that morning. Instead he'd thought of all the ways he wanted to make love to her.

For a man who'd been focused on revenge and corporate takeovers for most of his adult life, it had been unnerving to say the least. So he'd driven here to talk to her. To prove to himself that he'd remembered it all wrong. That she hadn't changed him by falling into his arms.

But that wasn't the way this was going.

Instead he was sitting at the kiddie table listening to the babble of three-year-olds and realizing two things. One, that if this was they were going to launch a reading app for this market, he was going to have to find a lot more patience for dealing with his future focus groups. And two, he was still just as attracted to Emma as he'd been the day before. In fact he might be even more so than he'd previously thought.

Never before had the way a woman nibbled a breakfast snack turned him on. But it had today.

"Is that okay?" she asked.

No, he thought. Then realized she had to be talking about something else. There was no way she could possibly know that she'd rattled him. "I'm sorry, what did you say?"

"I asked if you'd mind if Sammy and some of his

friends played with the prototype and then gave us some feedback."

"That's what I was going to suggest," he said. He glanced around the table and noticed that the kids had finished their snacks and were putting away their lunch boxes. It was just he and Emma sitting there.

He popped his last raisin into his mouth and then pushed up to his feet. He was more than ready to get out of the nursery. He hadn't been around this many kids since he'd been one himself. The merger and the relationships that had sprung up from it were making his life a mess, Kell thought. There were babies everywhere. Which made him think about things he'd never really considered before. Like the future.

Emma stood up as well, brushing her hands down the sides of her pantsuit and tucking the tail of her blouse back into the waistband where it had come out. Her long hair hung around her shoulders. His palms tingled with the remembered feel of its silkiness and he wanted to touch it again. Touch her again. He didn't know how he was going to keep his word that he wouldn't pursue her.

It was all he wanted.

It made no sense. He felt like an idiot. Why was he here? He should be running in the other direction instead of stopping by her office.

"Kell?"

"Yes?"

"You okay?"

No, he wasn't okay. In fact he to admit, he'd never been okay. He'd always been just a little messed up.

And part of that was due to his mom. He saw the way Emma was with Sammy, and couldn't help thinking that his own mom had never come and had a snack with him at school.

No matter how many times he'd told himself he hadn't expected her, he'd always sort of hoped she'd show up at something. But she never had.

Sammy was lucky to have Emma. And Kell knew that probably the best gift he could give the kid would be to make sure that Emma's job didn't take up too much of her time. He should fire her now, get her out of his life, give the kid his mom full-time and—

Pretty much piss off the only family he had. There were really only two people in the world that he'd always cared about, and they were Allan and Dec. If he fired Emma they'd be furious.

He was stuck.

It didn't matter that it was common sense to avoid the mess that was this five-foot, five inch, one-hundred-thirty-pound woman with reddish-brown hair and eyes that made him forget she was the granddaughter of his sworn enemy and the only person still alive who'd witnessed his greatest humiliation.

"Yes, I'm fine. Just realized that a focus group with kids is going to be very interesting," he said, trying to bring his mind back to business.

"I agree. I think we should give it to Jessi's team and see what they can do with it," Emma said with a grin.

"Your sister already doesn't like me, despite Allan's best efforts to change her mind. I think if I suggested that she should head up focus groups with three-year-olds she'd go ballistic."

Emma laughed. The sound was full and infectious and he couldn't help almost smiling. The fact that he never smiled was the only thing that kept him from doing it now.

"We can work out those details in your office," he said.

He wanted to get away from her son and this environment. He was seeing Emma as a person and not simply an employee in a company he'd taken over. She was no longer looking like collateral damage but like a woman. His woman.

No. She'd never be his and that was the only way it could be. And after today, he wasn't coming to the Malibu office.

He'd make Dec deal with Emma and her transition from now on. Kell had to keep his distance before he did something he'd totally regret like pull her back into his arms and kiss her yet again.

Emma took the stairs up to her office, not wanting to risk getting trapped in the elevator with Kell. Not this morning, when she was seeing him in the new light that had started yesterday. It was one thing to say their behavior in the elevator had been a fluke but to see him this morning, sitting on the floor and talking to her son, had made Kell seem like a regular guy. And that had put images in her head that she had no business believing. Images that made it seem as if maybe she could kiss him again and more.

Which was absolutely insane. He was still Kell Montrose. A man who was ruled by the past and determined to eradicate her from the face of gaming.

Was that his play?

Had he kissed her yesterday to set in motion the ultimate revenge? Make her fall for him and then either break her heart or get her to give up the Chandler legacy?

She groaned.

"You okay?" Kell asked as he trudged up the stairs behind her.

"Yes, just thinking about the huge task in front of me." Which was going to be twice as hard since she was dealing with these new ideas about Kell. It was easier to plan for her future without him in the picture as anything other than her mortal enemy.

Now everything was muddled.

The same way it had been when she met Helio. He'd swept her off her feet in a way that Kell never would or even could. But Helio had shaken up her neat little world and made her realize that all the truths she'd always held were fallible. And that scared her.

Helio's death had sent her scurrying and hiding in Infinity Games. She couldn't risk anything like that happening again. She had to remember that.

"It's going to be a challenge, but I have the feeling you like that," he said, as they reached the executive floor and stepped out into the carpeted hallway.

"I do," she admitted. "Plus there's the fact that you kind of expect me to fail. I'd love to prove you wrong."

"Would you?"

"Yes. I like winning," she said. "Your takeover knocked me down but I'm more than ready to get back up and go for it again."

"Good. It's no fun going into battle with an opponent you know you can beat."

"Truly? You thought you could beat me? Didn't dealing with Jessi show you anything?" she asked as she led the way to her office. She walked around behind her big walnut desk and started to sit down, but Kell had followed her and stood by the plate glass windows that overlooked a view of the Pacific Ocean.

"Jessi was unexpected," he admitted. "But you're more civilized."

"On the surface," she said. She'd learned early on that she accomplished more when people assumed she was agreeable and malleable; it had served her well in her career up to this point. But underneath she was just as determined and willing to go to any lengths as Jessi was. Jessi had courted a Hollywood producer and gotten them exclusive rights to develop a game based on his upcoming action movie. She just went about it in a different way.

"Stop it," he said.

"Stop what?"

"Getting more interesting. Could you please go back to being the all-business Emma—the woman I had never kissed and pretty much never thought of except for crushing you in the business arena."

She looked over at him and tucked this new tidbit away to use later. She wasn't ruthless…she honestly didn't believe all's fair in love and in war, because in those cases someone always got caught in the cross fire. But she did believe in using everything at her disposal to her advantage.

"You think I'm interesting."

He closed the gap between them in two long strides and put his hands on her waist. His touch was light, but his body language was aggressive, and she had the feeling that she'd just pushed him too far. Another tidbit she should tuck away.

She felt perfectly safe with him like this. She knew that he'd never hurt her—she didn't know why she was so certain but she was.

"I can't help being myself," she said, at last.

"You weren't like this last week."

"I was. You didn't notice," she said.

He pulled her toward him. "I'm pretty observant. I think I would have been aware that you were flirting with me."

"You think so?" she asked, tipping her head to the side.

He nodded.

She lifted one finger up to caress the line of his jaw and felt a tiny scar there. Where had he gotten it? One little flaw in an otherwise perfect face.

"What do you want me to say?"

"That you can survive a no-holds-barred sexual affair that has a built-in end date."

Shaken, she stared up into those pewter eyes of his, eyes that she knew she'd never look into again and think of as icy, because they burned with such a white-hot flame now. The rawness in his voice scared her.

What he wanted…well, she wanted it, too, but she was done leaping into affairs. She was done with trusting that the future would sort itself out—it never really did. She swallowed hard.

He cursed under his breath.

"Why flirt then?" he asked.

"I can't resist it. I know I should hold my tongue but I can't."

"I have a few ideas of what to do with your tongue," he said. "Give me a kiss, Emma. One last kiss just for this moment and then I'll let you go and you'll stop flirting with me and that will be it."

"One kiss? Wasn't that what started this craziness?" she asked, licking her lips because just the thought of kissing him made everything feminine inside of her go on high alert.

Four

Kell's rational brain was no longer in charge. He had nothing left to lose. He wanted her, he couldn't think when she was around and kissing her seemed like the most sensible thing in a world that had gone completely insane.

"Was it the kiss that started all this? I thought it was that time we worked together in the copy room more than ten years ago."

Her breath caught. "I didn't think you remembered that day."

"I don't really dwell on it that often but it's always in the back in my mind. I think that one incident set all of this into motion."

She kept running her finger along his jaw and it made it nearly impossible for him to think. But then holding her in his arms wasn't really helping to keep him focused either. There was something about Emma and there always had been. She was smart, pretty, funny and unattainable. Still. Even though he'd conquered her, taken over her company and put her in a position where he should be holding all the cards, she pulled out this sexiness that he'd never really noticed before.

And once again he was at the disadvantage.

"You were so good-looking back then. And there wasn't that edge to you that there is now."

"What edge?"

"Like you always have your guard up. Even now when you are asking me for a kiss…there's a dominance to you."

"Dominance suits me," he said. "Are you going to kiss me?"

"Not if you keep talking about it. We both know this is stupid," she said.

"I no longer care," he said. "I have your company, everyone on the board knows your plan to try to save your job. I am not going to make you promises of continued employment if you sleep with me. I'm just going to tell you that we both will sleep better if we do."

She shook her head and he wondered if he'd miscalculated but he knew he hadn't. He and Emma were similar. They always had been. They were the oldest of their families. The ones who'd been tasked with continuing the feud that their grandfathers had started. And they both were tired of carrying that mantle. Or at least he hoped she was.

Because he dreamed of kissing her mouth. Of tasting her one more time. He didn't want to just walk away, and this time he wasn't going to.

He still regretted letting her out of the elevator at Playtone-Infinity headquarters yesterday. It wasn't in his nature to deny himself anything he wanted.

He lowered his head. Knowing this might be the last chance, he tried to take his time. He rubbed his lips over hers; she opened her mouth on a gasp and the sweetness of her breath brushed over him. He traced the seam of her lips with his tongue before pulling her closer and plunging his tongue deeper.

Slow, his mind said. *Never,* his body replied. She was in his arms, and taking his time was the last thing he wanted to do. At war with himself he did the one thing he'd been wanting to do since he'd left her in the stairwell yesterday. He pulled her closer to him, forgot she was a Chandler and he a Montrose. He kissed her like she was just Emma, a girl he knew, unencumbered by their past.

Her fingers slid up his jaw to his neck and she held him lightly as he kissed her. The way she touched him sent chills down his spine and made him long for more than this one kiss could offer.

He'd never lost himself in an embrace like this before. He wanted to pretend that she wasn't different. That he wasn't different. But that was another lie.

He felt his erection stir and she shifted to rub her hips against him. He groaned and slipped his hand around to her back and tugged her blouse from the waistband until he could slide his hand under the fabric and touch her skin. He exposed just a few inches at the small of her back but it was more erotic than having some other woman totally naked.

Her skin was softer than he'd thought a woman's could be. She shivered a little at his touch and curled one hand tighter around his neck as she rose on tiptoe and deepened their kiss. He shook with the intensity of his need for her. He was still being subtle but his gut called for him to go for it.

He pushed one hand under her blouse and let his palm move slowly up between her shoulder blades, urging her closer to his chest. Her hands moved down his shoulders and he drew her closer as he continued to kiss her.

The he lifted her off her feet and turned to set her on her desk. He thrust his thigh between her legs and maneuvered them apart until he could stand between them. He felt the bite of her fingernails in his shoulders and lifted his head.

Her skin was flushed, her eyes half-closed and her lips parted as each breath was a forceful exhalation. Her hand came between them hovering over his chest before falling to touch him just over his racing heart.

"What are we doing?"

He didn't want to talk or think. Instead he traced the high line of her cheekbone and her long smooth neck with his fingertip before lowering his head to kiss her again.

She hesitated for a second before wrapping her arms around him and drawing him closer. Her tongue tangled with his before plunging deeper and deeper. He had never wanted a woman more.

Nothing seemed to matter but this moment in time and he wanted it to never end. Because he also knew that once it did, it wouldn't come again.

Kell's hands were moving with surety and purpose and she knew that if she was going to call this off she had to do it soon. But he felt good. His kiss tasted just right and in a world where everything had been wrong for so long she wanted to believe in this. But she knew she couldn't.

She groaned and pulled away from him. Saw that fiery passion in his pewter eyes and called herself a fool. But she'd rather stop herself now than regret this later. Hadn't she promised herself no more jumping and hoping the bridge would appear? Wasn't this just the kind of situation she had been trying to avoid?

She leaned forward, resting her forehead on his chest, and heard him curse savagely under his breath. Apologies danced around in her mind but she couldn't vocalize them just yet.

"I'm freaking out here," she said into his chest.

He awkwardly patted her on the back but she could tell he was still turned on. His breath was quick and labored and his erection pressed against her thigh. Stopping was at once the hardest thing she'd ever done and the most sensible. This was Kell Montrose.

Something her body didn't seem to give a care about.

"I shouldn't have—hell, I still want to. I can't say

I regret a single moment of it," he said. His voice had an edge that she'd previously only heard in the board-room when someone pissed him off.

"You said one kiss," she reminded him.

"I thought you wouldn't be able to stop," he admit-ted ruefully as he stepped away from her. He made no attempt to hide his hard-on as he put his hands on his hips and confronted her.

"Fear is the only thing stopping me, Kell," she said, feeling small and alone again. "I bet that's something you don't let rule you, but for me it's a constant."

"I get afraid sometimes," he admitted. "I can be cautious but I usually just go for it. I have nothing to lose here."

"And I have everything. It's not easy for me to call a halt to things but I'm not like I used to be."

"In what way?" he asked, shoving his hands through that thick hair of his, leaving it disheveled.

Her fingers actually tingled with the need to reach out and smooth his hair. God, she was a mess. She needed distance from Kell instead of more meetings.

"I'm just so aware of the consequences associated with risk now. I've become very cautious."

He nodded and walked around the desk to lean a hip on the front of it. "To your detriment. Your hesitancy left Infinity Games vulnerable to me and my takeover."

She chewed her lower lip as the truth of what he said sank in. Helio's death had changed her, taken her to the edge and left her a hollow shell of who she used to be. These last few months when she'd been scrapping with Kell had been good for her but she was still scared.

"That's the difficulty. I can't live the way I used to and you've shaken things up and made me realize that I have to change. But an affair with you isn't sensible. It would complicate things."

"Who said it has to be an affair? I'd be happy with a one-night stand," he said, wriggling his eyebrows at her and giving her a cocky grin.

"You said that about a kiss and it wasn't enough," she said carefully.

"That's right. I did," he said, crossing over to one of the guest chairs and sitting down on it. He leaned forward, putting his elbows on his knees, and stared at the floor for a minute.

She was reminded again of how human he was beneath the corporate robot image that she'd had of him. He wasn't an automaton. He was a guy trying to figure out life the same way she was. They'd both been screwed by their family legacy, the feud that could be put down to greed on one side and bitterness on the other. There had been no winners, even in their generation. Not unless you counted her sisters and his cousins.

"If I thought there was even half a chance we could be intimate and still work together, I think I'd go for it," she said, but that was a lie. She knew it as soon as the words left her mouth. Kell made her feel again. And if she'd learned one thing from losing Helio, it was that she didn't want to be that emotionally dependent on anyone again. Sammy and her sisters were the very limit of whom she could care about. Her sisters' new babies were already making her feel uncomfortable because she worried about them. Like Hannah's fever last week that had been so high for so long. Luckily they'd finally gotten it lower after a few hours in the hospital.

She'd been on the edge then. Worrying for her sister Jessi and for little Hannah…it had served to remind her of how fragile life was.

Fragile. Dammit, it was. Should she really give up a chance to be in Kell's arms because it might not end well when she knew that no one was guaranteed a tomorrow?

There was a knock on the door, then it opened and Jessi walked in. "Sorry. I didn't know you were in a meeting."

"Come on in," Kell said. "We have a task for you."

Emma bit the inside of her cheek to keep from smiling as Jessi hesitated to come any further.

"What kind of task?"

"Focus group. That's right up your alley, isn't it?"

"Yes," she said. "Why'd you say it so ominously? You like messing with me, don't you," Jessi said. She wore her dark hair in a bob that was longer in the front than in the back and had a thick fall of bangs that covered one eye.

"We want you to do it with a group of three-year-olds," Kell said. "Emma will give you the details later."

"What?"

"I will talk to you about it later," Emma said. "Can you give us a few more minutes?"

"What?"

"Go," Emma said.

Jessi left the office muttering under her breath.

Emma saw the hint of a smile on Kell's face and it

made something melt inside of her. "Let's talk business, but then tonight…do you want to come to dinner at my place?"

"What?"

"Now you sound like Jessi."

"Okay. I'll come to dinner," he said.

Kell showed up early to dinner at Emma's house not because he was anxious. Of course he wasn't anxious. He was a man who had everything, so dinner at the posh beachfront Malibu mansion should be routine for him and he knew it.

He'd tried telling himself that what he felt for her was simply sexual but this entire situation was beginning to make him feel as if he was losing his marbles. He knew better than to believe this was something he couldn't live without. He'd learned a long time ago that life—his life—was meant to be lived solo.

But when he found someone he wanted to spend part of his journey with, he went for it. He'd seen how bitter Grandfather Thomas had become throughout his life, not just because of the soured business deal with the Chandlers, but also because his obsession with getting back at Gregory Chandler had cost him his wife and then his son. The old man had believed that a Chandler had stolen everything.

As Kell sat in front of Emma's house he wondered how much of his attraction to her was lust and how much could be attributed to something so much simpler. Something that looked like revenge for the old man. And he knew that having dinner with her was dumb. This entire crazy lust thing was even stupider. He wasn't a fool.

Why then was he suddenly acting like one?

It would be easy to say that seeing his cousins pair up with Emma's sisters was at the root of it. And he'd be lying if he denied that it was hard to always be the single guy at their get-togethers. But he could easily avoid them.

And then become his bitter, lonely old grandfather. Something he had never wanted to become. When had everything gotten so complicated?

He'd had it all a few short months ago but revenge had proven more complicated than just getting back at his enemy.

It brought with it emotions that Kell hadn't counted on.

He got out of his Porsche 911 and walked to the front door. He'd brought a small gift for Sammy and nothing for Emma. Which was part of his fooling himself that this wasn't a date but more a research excursion to find out what kids wanted from games.

But that was a lie, too.

God, he was really getting into self-delusion these days.

But he wasn't. Lust wasn't something new to him. He'd been wanting what the Chandlers had for as long as he could remember. So it wasn't a huge surprise that he wanted Emma. In fact, given the perverse way his mind worked, it was to be expected.

He knocked on the front door and heard the sound of wheels on a tile floor. Then the door opened.

"Hiya," Sammy said. The toddler didn't look a lot like Emma, instead Kell saw a strong resemblance to Helio Cerventes, the Formula 1 driver who'd been his father.

"Hiya. Can I come in?"

"You sure can," Emma said, coming up behind her son. She wore a pair of cream-colored leggings and a long sweater in a soft pink color that ended at the middle of thighs. She had a pair of dinosaur slippers on her feet.

He arched one eyebrow at her and she shrugged. "Sammy gave them to me for Christmas."

"Good choice."

"Thanks," Sammy said with a big grin. "Want to race?"

Kell glanced at Emma and she nodded. "He means around the house. Him in the car, you running."

"Is there time for that?"

"As a matter fact, you can do one lap while I pour you a drink. What would you like, Kell?"

"What are you drinking?"

"Corona Light with lime. We're having fajitas for dinner."

"Sounds great. Where's the start line?" he asked Sammy.

The little boy got back into his black two-seater coupe. It looked like a Mercedes; Kell recalled that Helio had driven for Team Mercedes. He also noticed that Emma had a device in her hand.

"What's that?"

"Remote control. In case Sammy gets into trouble."

"Mommy is the start line," Sammy said.

"Maybe we should do a run through so...what do you want Sammy to call you? Kell or Mr. Montrose or Mr. Kell."

"No," Sammy said.

"What do you mean no?"

"Auntie Jessi calls him Darth. Like *Star Wars*."

Emma turned three different shades of red. Kell, who'd heard a few of Jessi's more unflattering names for him, wasn't surprised by the Darth Vader reference.

"Kell is fine."

"Good. Follow me and I'll show you the route you'll be racing on," she said.

Sammy maneuvered around them and led the way down the wide open hallway into the kitchen, around the breakfast table into a great room and then back to the entryway.

"Think you got it?"

This was the last thing he'd expected to do tonight and it put all of his thoughts into perspective. It was hard to take yourself too seriously when you were faced with a competition with a three-year-old. As Emma dropped her hands and told them to go, Kell realized it was exactly the sort of experience that had been missing from his life.

Sammy drove quickly and expertly around the curves, impressing Kell. As they closed in on the final stretch and he saw Emma waiting and smiling, he realized that it didn't matter if he won or lost, if this was smart or dumb. He was just glad he was here.

Five

After they ate, Emma put Sammy to bed and rejoined Kell on the patio, where she'd left him. Dinner had been interesting and far more tense than she would have imagined it could be. Kell tried but was clearly out of his element with her son. Not only that: it was soon clear that she and Kell were opposites on everything that mattered.

Politics, books, movies, even games. There was no middle ground between them. They were both passionate about their opinions. She realized that their upbringing had to be one of their main influences and she wondered how their grandfathers—hers the financially driven man and his the high-concept dreamer—had ever put aside their different ideologies to start their own company.

"I guess I should be going," Kell said when she re-joined him. He'd made a fire in the fire pit for them.

It was one of the things that she always struggled with. She just wasn't good at it. And Kell seemed pretty good at everything he tried.

"I think so. I had no idea that we'd have nothing in common between us," she said. She'd never been one to ignore the obvious and had a tendency to just state things even though it might be prudent to keep her mouth shut. She worked hard to keep the filter in place while she was at work but here at her home when the evening had gone so horribly not to plan, she didn't feel like it.

"Me either. Interesting what we do have in common though—sex and video games," he said.

"Sounds like the title of a bad movie," she said. And that was all that it would be. She had seen him strug-gling with Sammy as the toddler got in and out of his booster seat. There were things that singletons would never really understand about parenting until they had a child of their own.

Sammy was so much a part of her life that she couldn't have someone in it who didn't understand him or his needs.

"I'm sorry," he said.

"Me too," she admitted. "It started out so well when you let Sammy win the race."

"Let him? That kid has the makings of a fine driver someday. Did you see the way he instinctively acceler-ated out of the turns?"

"Unfortunately, yes. My father-in-law is already

anxious to get him racing go-karts. But I don't want that for him or for myself if I'm honest."

"You're a good mom," he said out of the blue. "It would make me crazy to do what you do. I have no idea how you manage it all."

"I don't manage it very well. As you pointed out, I did lose my company," she said.

"But given the handicap you were playing with... I'm not sure I would have gotten it so easily if Sammy hadn't been in the picture," Kell said.

"Thanks, I think. I'm glad I do have my son. He's the reason I wanted Infinity Games to succeed," she said.

"It will. Even if you no longer have a position in the company, your shares will still earn a nice profit. It will always be a part of his legacy."

She walked around the patio, stopping to look out over the railing. The beach was dark, the sound of the surf a distant rolling sound. Legacy. That was the purview of men usually. But as she'd been the oldest Chandler it had fallen to her. She wanted to pretend it didn't matter but she knew that was a big lie.

It mattered a lot.

It hurt her that she'd let her grandfather's hard work slip from her fingers into the hands of his enemy. And with that realization came the fact that she'd made to-night into a nightmare by trying to find the ways they were different.

She didn't want to have anything in common with Kell and the truth was she did have a lot in common with him.

"You okay?" he asked, coming over to her. He was an intense man but when he was quiet there was almost a peacefulness about him.

Considering he'd spent the better part of his life seeped in bitterness and questing for revenge, it was odd. "How come you're almost normal?"

He laughed. "*Almost* being the key word, right?"

"No, I mean it. I'm facing the hard truth that I've been difficult tonight because I guess I'm a bit of a brat."

"Just a bit?" he asked, with a teasing lilt in his voice.

She looked over at him, with his thick dark hair and fallen angel features, and understood why she'd put so many barriers in place between them. He'd be too easy to fall for. Not just because of his hot, sexy body, but because he was successful and driven and understood the time she had to spend at the office. Not many men would.

"Maybe more than a bit. But I wasn't expecting you to be so...."

"Normal?" he asked. "That's not exactly a compliment."

"Who said I was trying to compliment you," she said. "Your ego is healthy enough without me feeding it."

"That's true. No use pretending I'm not all that."

She shook her head because he was being flippant and she couldn't blame him. "When did you figure out that I was being difficult?"

"When you argued in favor of sparkling vampires. I get the fact that the *Twilight* romance triangle appealed to you but that you actually liked sparkly men…well, that was too farfetched."

She laughed. "Sorry. I'm contrary by nature. I try so hard to be easygoing and get along with everyone else, but with you I always have to take the opposite viewpoint."

"I noticed. It's not the worst quality I've encountered on a first date," he said.

She led the way to one of the padded benches and sat down. He followed and sat down next to her, stretching his arm along the back of the couch. "What was the worst?"

"The woman who asked for my social security number so she could run a background check on me before we left the restaurant. You?"

"No horror stories, really. Though in college I had a date who invited me to a wet T-shirt contest."

"Nice. Why didn't I think of that?" Kell asked.

"Um…I declined and poured my drink on him," Emma said.

"I bet that would have been something to see."

"I could dump my drink on you if you're interested," she said with a smile.

"I meant you in a wet T-shirt."

And just like that she knew why she'd been pushing so hard for the distance between them. It hadn't just been because of her contrariness but because she'd been running from this attraction.

The evening hadn't gone according to plan. Emma was different than he'd expected. And it hadn't been just the way she'd argued with him on every topic he'd brought up. Clearly she had been sending him a message that she didn't want to get involved and he'd received it.

But he'd also seen the love she had for her son. Being a mother was important to her and that had touched something deep inside of him. A part of himself that he didn't realize he'd even had. He had never really had any kind of female role model growing up. It had just been Grandfather and him. His aunt Helene had been bitter once she'd realized her dream marriage had been arranged so that her husband could access her inheritance. And Allan's mom didn't like her father so they'd never seen her.

But right now all of that seemed unimportant. Right now he was picturing full-chested Emma in a wet T-shirt contest. He applauded her long ago boyfriend for his idea even though it had cost him the date.

"Why are we so attracted to each other?" she asked under her breath, so he knew she didn't expect an answer.

It was something that he'd pondered himself. There wasn't a more inconvenient woman to be lusting after than this one. Everything about her was difficult from her last name to her circumstances. But he was fixated on her. And the more he uncovered about her, the more attractive she became.

"Fate?" he suggested. "The ultimate joke on our grandfathers and on us."

"Really? What about free will?"

"The way you are putting up barriers, I'd say that free will is definitely one up on fate."

"Nothing worth having comes easily," she said.

"Which is why I'm still here," he said, putting his hand on her shoulder.

"Oh, is that the reason why?" she asked. "I thought it was because you were determined to have the evening go your way."

"I am. But I'd never be so crass as to say it. I might not have grown up with a mom but I know better than that."

She tipped her head to the side, staring at him with that intense gaze of hers that made him hope he was good enough. "What happened with your mom?"

"I can't…I don't want to talk about it."

She nodded, then tucked one leg under her body and turned to face him. "When my parents died in the car crash I felt such a gaping emptiness and I almost gave into it. Then I noticed my sisters standing next to me at the funeral and they were lost, too, and I had to pull it together for them.

"If it wasn't for them I don't know how I would have coped. We had each other. Did you have anyone?"

He pushed himself to his feet and paced away from her. "I don't want to talk about this. Ever."

She came over to him and put her hand in the center of his back. There was something about her touch that calmed all the anger that his past always stirred in him. But he knew it was false. She was playing him.

She had to be.

Nothing else made sense.

He turned and pulled her into his arms. Then he brought his mouth down on hers, intent on showing that the only thing he wanted from her was physical. But as the kiss continued, anger drained from him and he was once again caught in the quagmire that was Emma. She changed him, and he didn't want that. But there was no keeping her from doing it.

She wrapped her arms around his shoulders and he lifted her off her feet by leaning back. He liked the feel of her body pressed wholly to his. Breast-to-chest, stomach-to-stomach, erection to the perfect softness of her body.

He knew now exactly why he'd stayed. What he'd wanted since the first moment they'd been alone and he'd been the clear victor. No more games or waiting. He had come here tonight because he wanted to move beyond the thought that this attraction was taking over his life.

Once he had her, once he'd made her his completely, life would go back to normal. He wasn't hesitating anymore. He'd put up with a lot of nonsense from her and now it was time—

"Kell?"

"Yes?" he asked, lifting his mouth from hers and dropping nibbling kisses down the line of her neck.

"I—"

He groaned.

How many times was he going to be stopped by her conscience, and why was he so determined to keep going after her when she clearly wanted to wait? She deserved him to stop pushing but he wanted her worse than he'd craved any other woman in his life.

She shook her head. "I'm not saying no. Just that I need to make sure I have the baby monitor out here. I don't want Sammy to interrupt us."

"Me either," he admitted. "Should I go?"

"No," she said. "We need to get this lust thing out of the way and see if there is anything else between us besides a decades-old rivalry."

"I agree."

Agreeing didn't lessen the fear in the pit of her stomach. She wanted him and wasn't about to send him away but there was a big part of her that already knew this was a mistake. But one she wanted: she wasn't about to deny herself the pleasure of Kell.

She'd been running on empty and sustaining herself as a woman on old memories. Kell was warm, solid, real and so damned sexy it made her ache when he held her in his arms.

She took his hand and led him toward the house but he stopped.

"Where's your bedroom?"

"Why?" she asked.

"I'll put this fire out and give you a moment to make sure Sammy is settled and then meet you."

It made sense. And a part of her wondered if Kell was afraid like her. Then she laughed at herself. What man was afraid of sex?

"Top of the stairs, second door on the left. I'll leave it open," she said.

He nodded and she walked into her house, making sure the nightlights she used downstairs were on, and then made her way up to Sammy's nursery, which was next to her bedroom. He was sleeping soundly in his toddler bed that was shaped like a racecar. She looked down on him and felt that same surge of love she always did.

He made her life so full. But even so, there was always something missing. It wasn't that she had to have a man in her life, but there were times when she was reminded she was still a young woman with needs.

She pulled Sammy's door partially closed after she'd adjusted the monitor so she'd have a clear view and then went into her bedroom. She turned the receiver on so she could see him and then flicked on the light beside the bed and turned down the covers.

And then...waited. She'd never been a femme fatale and nothing had happened to change that. She felt awkward, and by the time Kell showed up in the doorway she had had second and third thoughts about this.

He gave her a wry grin.

"Too much time to think?"

"Something like that," she said.

"Let me help you out." He walked into her bedroom, taking his iPhone out of his pocket and placing it on the dresser. Then he fiddled with it for a second before she heard the smooth sounds of Ella Fitzgerald singing "Feeling Good."

He turned and opened his arms to her and she stepped closer and into them. This was what she needed. When they touched there was not time for doubts or worries. Or for anything other than his touch and the way he made her feel. They swayed to the music and she realized that it was a new night for them.

A chance to at last put the past to rest and figure out what their new dynamic would be. Work would sort itself out and they'd get to the bottom of this unexpected thing between them.

"This is the kind of music you like, right?" he asked.

"Yeah. I'm kind of dorky about things like that," she said.

"You don't seem too dorky to me," he said, sweeping his hands down her back to her hips and then pulling her closer so that she was pressed against the cradle of his thighs. His mouth came down on hers as the music changed to Louis Prima, and the rough sound of the music felt like the perfect backdrop to this embrace with Kell.

It gave the evening an unreal aspect, as if she were starring in her own classic Hollywood movie and there would be no consequences from this that she couldn't figure out on her own. Kell tasted of lime and Corona as he kissed her and she tipped her head farther back to allow him to deepen the kiss.

They knew each other well enough now that they both opened their mouths at the same time and their tongues tangled together in a rush of hot breath. She rubbed her hands down his back to his waistband and pulled his shirt free of his pants.

He was sliding his hands under the hem of her long sweater and cupping her butt as he thrust against her. She loved it and swiveled her hips against him.

She felt the world spin around her as he lifted her off her feet and carried her to her bed. He placed her in the center but on the edge so that her thighs hung over the side. She pushed herself up on her elbows and watched as he slowly unbuttoned his shirt and then cast it aside.

His chest was lightly dusted with hair and his pecs were well developed. His stomach was smooth but not rock hard and in her mind he was perfect. She felt a rush of moisture between her legs as excitement spread through her.

He pulled his belt off and tossed it on the floor next to his shirt, then tipped his head to the side. "I'm feeling a little underdressed here."

"Not nearly enough," she said. "I had no idea that you were so muscular."

"Do you like it?" he asked, flexing his biceps. "It's L.A., baby, you have to work out or you feel like a schlub."

"Well it's working for you," she said.

He took a step forward, putting his hands on her thighs and drawing her hips to the edge of the bed. Then he grabbed the bottom of her sweater and pulled it up over her head, tossing it aside.

She glanced down at herself, at her average breasts in a bra, which luckily was new. A pretty light pink one with brown polka dots on it. He reached down and traced the demi-cups and the flesh that they didn't cover. Then he slid the strap off her left shoulder and leaned down to kiss it.

Six

Her bedroom was like everything else about Emma: a complicated contradiction. He'd expected it to be sleek and modern but the furniture was antique in the old-world style. Her dresser was covered in photos of her family and on the wall above the bed there was a rustic wooden shutter with the words *She turned her can'ts into cans and her dreams into plans* on it.

She lay in front of him with her breasts rising with each breath she took, her legs on either side of his and her eyes watching him with anticipation. He wanted to pretend she was any woman, to not see her as Emma, but that was impossible. She was Emma from the top of her reddish-brown hair, which fell in soft waves over her shoulders, to the pink and brown bra that covered her breasts.

"What are you waiting for?" she asked.

He wanted to savor this moment. He had learned that things he really treasured rarely came into his life more than once. "No need to rush this."

He was glad for the shadows in the room; they suited him. He didn't allow himself to think; instead he just focused on her body and his reaction to it.

Her hair spread out on the comforter behind her head as she propped herself up on her elbows. She parted her thighs a little further apart and slid one hand down her body over her rib cage to her belly button and then glanced up at him.

"If you're not going to touch me…."

He climbed up on the bed and pulled her into his arms, drawing her over him. Her hands were trapped between them and he felt her fingers on his chest moving slowly over him.

"I like the way your chest hair tickles my fingers," she said, shifting on his lap.

She bit his earlobe and whispered all the things that she wanted him to do to her. The erotic talk turned him on, painted images in his mind of things that he couldn't wait for them to do.

He cupped her butt and pulled her forward, drawing her up so that her breasts were level with his face. She wrapped her arms around his head and drew him closer as he quickly dispensed with her bra and nibbled and kissed his way from one breast to the other. He traced the outline of her nipple and then lightly scraped his teeth over it.

She shifted her shoulders and looked down at him.

He glanced up from where his face was buried in her chest and she bit her lower lip. He cupped both of her breasts, felt them swell under his hands, and then he pinched one nipple lightly while he sucked the other nipple deep into his mouth. He swirled his tongue around it and felt her rock forward against him.

Her hands sprawled out on his back as she pulled him closer and closer to her. He held her to him with one hand in the middle of her back. She rotated her shoulders and he was surrounded by the scent of her, the feel of her, the sensuality of her. He was so hard and hot, he was going to explode, but at the same time he used his iron self-control to slow down.

This night was going to last forever. He rolled so that they were next to each other on the bed and he could caress her entire body. He started with her arm, which he lightly stroked, and felt the goose bumps spread on her skin. He drew her hand up to his mouth and kissed the center of her palm and then put her hand on his chest.

She spread her fingers out and lightly rubbed circles over the muscles of his pectorals. It tickled, which startled a laugh from him.

"No." He caught her close and rolled her underneath him.

"Ah, did I find a weakness?" she asked with a carefree grin and he was struck by how beautiful her smile was. He leaned down and kissed her fiercely, holding her head in his hands.

"No. I don't have weaknesses."

"Sure you don't," she said, running her fingers

down his sides again, making him grab her wrists. He stretched her hands up above her head and held her underneath him.

She was just smiling as she rocked her hips against his and he felt her slide against his erection. This was so right. He had no idea why. The thought that this was Emma Chandler and he had no business being in her bed surfaced, but he shoved that aside.

He held her wrists in one hand and lowered his mouth to hers. He wasn't just teasing now, but determined to ensure she knew she was his. For tonight at least she belonged to him and he was going to claim every inch of her body.

He thrust his tongue deep into her mouth and felt her suck hard on his tongue as she arched underneath him. Her hard nipples poked into his chest and her legs scissored underneath his as he settled into the cradle of her thighs.

Caressing his way down her body with one hand, he found the waistband of her leggings and shoved them down her legs to the top of her thighs and let his hand move over from her thigh to her abdomen and then lower.

Her feminine center was hot, and as he traced her through her panties she moaned his name and arched against him. But now that he had her stretched out beneath him he found the control he'd almost lost.

He palmed her and then pulled the fabric of her underwear from her body, sweeping one finger down until he heard her breath catch. Then he lightly caressed her nub of desire. Slowly at first, with just a light back and forth motion, until she started to move restlessly against him.

Then he pushed his finger lower and found the moist opening of her body and slid it inside. He felt her hips jerk and she pulled her mouth from him.

"More."

Her breathless voice was like a caress on his spine. His pants felt even tighter and he wished he'd striped them both naked. But this was nice. It felt so good as he pressed his thumb to her clitoris and let his finger thrust in and out of her body.

She was hot and wet and so damned ready for him.

He kept up his caresses until he felt her hips moving more quickly against him. Then her body tightened as she dug her heels into the bed and thrust upward against his hand. He kept his fingers where they were, moving between her legs for a few more moments, and then drew his hand out of her panties and rolled to his side.

He pulled her leggings and underwear down her legs and tossed them on the floor and then stood up to take off his own pants. She lay on the bed watching him with languid eyes. Her skin was flushed, her breasts rising and falling rapidly, and her legs moved restlessly against the covers on the bed.

He crawled back over her and lowered himself slowly, using his entire body to caress hers. He eased his chest up over her torso and then slid his hands under her back to her butt and held his own weight on his forearms as he lowered himself until they were pressed together. She felt better than any other woman ever had before. It was so much more than he'd expected and he buried his head in her neck as emotions that he'd always kept locked away washed over him.

She wrapped her arms around him and held him close. For a minute they lay there until his erection reminded him he was holding a very naked, very tempting Emma in his arms and maybe he should do something about it.

He lifted his head and kissed her neck, nibbling at that point where it met her shoulder and her pulse beat so erratically. He felt it skip a beat as he sucked at her skin, then soothed the small area with his tongue before moving down her collarbone to her shoulder.

He learned her slowly with his hands and his mouth. He found a small birthmark under her left breast and caressed it with his tongue before moving lower over her ribs.

He found the small scar at her bikini line and when he looked up at her, she shrugged. "C-section."

He laved it with his tongue and felt her hands in his hair, tightening as he moved lower. Her inner thighs were sensitive to his touch and she twitched on the bed as he continued moving lower. He lingered there, kissing her, surrounded by her silky thighs and the scent of her passion. He couldn't resist turning his head and licking her center, tasting her.

She was addicting and he brought his mouth back to her more fully so he could thrust his tongue into her. Then he pulled back when she thrust her hands into his and drew him up.

"I can't take much more. I need you inside of me. Now."

He shifted away to reach for his pants and the condom he'd optimistically put in his pocket earlier. He sheathed himself quickly and then crawled back over her, but she put her hand in the middle of his chest and shoved him onto his back.

He rolled over and she climbed on top of him, reaching between her own legs to position him at her center. Then she braced herself on his chest and slowly lowered herself onto him. She moved so slowly that he thought he'd died and gone to heaven.

She slid him all the way inside of her body and then started to move on top of him. He brought his hands up to cup her breasts and caressed them as she moved over him. She reached behind her and put her hands on the top of his thighs, shifting her angle and taking him deeper into her body.

He held her by the waist as he felt her start to tighten around him. He thrust up into her harder and faster, taking every inch of her. Claiming, and being claimed in return.

Their eyes met and held as she bit her lower lip and leaned forward, riding him harder and faster. As the first wave of her orgasm rocked through her, he kept thrusting, pulling her down toward him to capture her nipple in his mouth, sucking deeply as he continued driving into her until he felt that tingling at the base of his spine that signaled his own orgasm.

He thrust into her three more times and she collapsed against him. Her entire body covered his, her hair tangling over his face as he held her closer, breathing in her scent. Realizing that everything in his world had changed.

Not because of the revenge he'd finally exacted on the Chandlers but because of this moment. He had thought he wasn't the kind of man who cared for anyone but he knew that was a lie as he turned his head away and cuddled Emma closer.

He cared for her.

He had a weakness he hadn't counted on and he had no idea how he was going to counteract it because a man with this kind of weakness made stupid mistakes.

Emma was exhausted. She felt her heart beat throughout her entire body as Kell sat up and lifted her off of him, setting her next to him on the bed. "I gotta clean up."

He walked toward the bathroom, which was marked with a pretty French sign that Cari had given her for Christmas last year. She watched his naked body as he walked away from her and came down from the physical high she'd been on.

Something was wrong.

He closed the door and she lay there for a second, knowing she should get up and put on her robe or something. But she was too perplexed by everything that had happened. When Kell had touched her C-section scar, she'd been forced to acknowledge that he was the first man to see her body post-baby, as Helio had died while she'd been pregnant. She'd been worried about

KATHERINE GARBERA   77

that after she'd first had Sammy but as time went on she'd changed.

Her priorities had gone from her obsession with how her body looked to the fact that if she did invite a man into her bed he was going to have to measure up in other areas.

She groaned and put her hands over her eyes as she felt an emotional release of all the things she'd been holding inside for too long. Kell Montrose was the first man she'd had sex with in four long years. And he'd shaken her to her core.

Physically, she couldn't have asked for more. He'd taken her to the limits of what she'd expected and pushed her beyond. Emotionally, he'd withdrawn. Something had happened at the end there and she knew that she had made a really stupid mistake.

Dammit, she was a smart woman. But why was it that when a man was dangerous to her she couldn't resist him? Kell was nothing like Helio but he had the power to wreak more havoc in her life than Helio had.

She rolled over and walked to her armoire, where she kept the television, and turned it on for the noise it provided. Her robe was on the back of the door in the bathroom so that wasn't available to her. Instead she grabbed her nightshirt from the top drawer in her dresser and then moved to the bed.

She had no experience at this kind of thing. She and Helio had both been in love from the moment their eyes met. She and Kell had been in conflict from birth, despite the fact that much of what she'd felt for him had changed in the past two days. She had no idea if it had for him.

In fact, given the hasty retreat he'd made to the bathroom she had to guess it hadn't.

She swallowed hard and tried to marshal her feelings into some sort of sensible order. But she felt a tinge of anger. He'd come over here, acting like a hot and horny Romeo, with a gift for her kid even, and now she felt as if she'd made a mistake by letting him into her bed.

She poured herself a glass of water from the pitcher that her housekeeper, Mrs. Hawking, kept filled on the nightstand for her. She wanted to curl up and hide but her days of retreat were long behind her. Some of her earliest memories were of standing up for herself and her sisters against their father's rants. She'd never been one to cower and she certainly wasn't going to be that way now. She gathered the clothing that was spread all over her bedroom floor and wondered how something that had felt so wonderful and right could have turned wrong.

She'd never have the answer because Kell was a man and his mind was unfathomable to her. She'd been surer of how to deal with him when they'd been enemies. But they technically weren't rivals anymore. They were family now. Even if she was fired from the company, their futures were inexplicably entwined.

And she'd slept with him. But more than that, she'd invited him into her home to meet her son and see her without any of the barriers that she used to protect herself in the workplace.

God, how was she going to face him for the rest of their lives knowing that he'd seen her naked and afterward had run? She knew that was his vulnerability showing and in no way a reflection on her. But it sure as hell felt a lot like rejection.

A lot like she hadn't measured up.

Considering she'd only shared her body with two other men, it hurt a lot.

She wanted to pretend that these things happened and she could shrug it off but she knew she couldn't. She'd been naked in front of him and he'd run away as soon as he'd....

Gotten what he wanted?

Not gotten it? She knew he'd come so it had nothing to do with the physical side of things.

What if he was as emotionally wrecked as she was? He said he'd grown up only with his grandfather and from what she'd seen of him he wasn't exactly good at relationships.

Anger was fading as she started to wonder if he was hiding in her bathroom. But that was dumb. When had Kell Montrose ever hid from anything? Never. He'd even let her grandfather humiliate him so that he could learn how to run a games company. Maybe that hadn't been his intention but Emma had always suspected that Kell had taken her grandfather's disdain as the price he had to pay to learn about gaming from the inside out.

She heard the door open and turned to see him standing on the threshold. She realized that she knew even less about him now that they'd been so intimate than ever before.

He didn't say anything as he stood there. He'd turned the lights in the bathroom off so only the flickering light from the television revealed him. She really couldn't read his expression or see him that well, but one thing was certain: something had changed in him. Something that felt as though it should be important but that she was afraid to believe in.

Seven

Kell knew that Emma was trouble from the first moment they'd met. He hadn't planned on sleeping with his longtime enemy but he had. Now he was paying the price. He wasn't the best when it came to relationships but he did know that a guy couldn't have soul-sex with a woman and then just walk out.

Not only was that death to the relationship—wait a minute, was this a relationship? Was that what he wanted? He felt as if he was on dangerous new ground and had no idea what to do next.

He'd spent too long in the bathroom staring into the mirror over the sink and hoping he'd see something other than his reflection, but he'd still been the same guy he'd always been. Someone who just didn't seem to feel emotions the way other people did.

The plan he'd concocted in the bathroom as he'd washed up seemed stupid now. There were no two ways about it. Faking a casual feeling he didn't feel wasn't going to work. For one thing he'd never been built that way. He wasn't any good at pretending.

He stood there feeling awkward and it had nothing to do with his nakedness. It had to do with letting Emma down easy. Even though he knew that she didn't love him, it was impossible for her reaction to be anything other than a type of heartbreak.

She didn't give herself easily or cheaply the way he did. He'd made love to a lot of woman without ever feeling a single thing for most of them. But Emma had that soft look in her eyes that told him she was starting to let herself care for him.

"Are you going to say something?"

"I'm not sure what to say," he admitted, rubbing his hand over his chest and walking farther into the room. She'd folded his clothes and put them on the end of the bed. He found his boxer briefs and pulled them on and then turned to face her, hands on his hips.

"We both know that I'm not the man you'd pick to sleep with," he said at last.

"Yet here you are in my bedroom," she said, trying for a lightness that failed.

"Indeed. I'm not sure if I should apologize. Hell, Em, I'm not sure at all what to do."

She sat up, curling one leg underneath her and leaning forward. "Talk to me. Tell me what's going on."

He wanted to share—no, he didn't. He wanted to

beat a hasty retreat but turning tail and running away wasn't part of his make-up any more than faking it was.

"You've confused me," he said.

"Good."

"Good?"

"Yes, it's about time I figured out how to shake the great Kell Montrose."

"Is that what this is about?" he asked. Was she playing some kind of game with him to get some sort of intimate revenge given that he'd taken over her company?

She shook her head and tipped her head down a little, breaking eye contract with him. "I wish. Then I'd be able to just wave toward the door and tell you to hit the road."

"But you want me to stay?"

He turned away from her, shoving his hands in his hair. Should he want to stay? Was that the proper thing? He'd had affairs, so he shouldn't feel this conflicted. This attached. But he did.

She was different. She was complicated. Ugh!

"I don't know," he admitted, turning back to face her.

"Then leave," she said. "It can just be sex."

It would never just be sex. He'd be haunted by this night and the way she'd made him feel, by the emotions she'd awakened, for the rest of his life. He knew it. He could deny it and make a break for it. Leave Malibu and go back to his chic apartment in downtown L.A. Or he could man up and face this. Face her and all the tough implications that sleeping with his enemy brought for him.

Because he couldn't separate the sexy woman who set fire to his body and his soul with the deep-seated hatred he held for the Chandlers.

"I don't think so," he said at last.

He couldn't help but think that his entire world was going to be shaped by this. He'd thought that if they slept together he'd be able to clear his head. Stop the fantasies and random sexy images that had been popping up at uncomfortable times. But he'd been wrong. So damned wrong.

"I'm making a hash of this."

"You are. But I think it's safe to say that our situation is odd to begin with. Our pasts are so entwined that it's hard to separate that and think of a future where we could be anything other than strained friends."

"Is that what you think?" he asked.

"I really don't know what to think. I haven't slept with a man since Helio and I am feeling more chaotic than I'd like to. One minute I want to cry, the next I want to yell, and tied up in that—in the middle—is you. Kell Montrose. The man who took everything I built in the last four years and tore it to the ground."

Her words were stark and honest. She didn't cower or hide or pretend that this wasn't one of the craziest things that either of them had ever found themselves facing.

"Fair enough. I'm the same way. I suck at relationships and have no idea how to act now."

"There isn't an etiquette book for this," she said. "There's no right or wrong way to behave."

"There is, though. Women have an unspoken checklist in their heads and a guy is left guessing what it is and how he should act," he said.

"Do you want to stay?" she asked again.

He looked at her sitting at the head of her bed with one leg curled underneath her, her hair tangled around her shoulders and a faded Philadelphia Eagles T-shirt on, and felt his answer in his gut.

"Yes."

She let out the breath that she hadn't realized she'd been holding. Then she moved around on her bed and pulled back the covers, opening them toward him as she slid underneath them.

He hesitated again and she wondered why. He'd said he didn't know how to react, and she remembered the things she knew about his upbringing. The comments her sisters had made about how bitter Thomas Montrose had always been and how his influence on his grandsons had left them broken. It was clear to her that Kell hadn't grown up surrounded by people who loved and cared for him. The stories of old Thomas had painted him as a bitter man.

She tried to steel her heart because she wanted to fix him. She was a fixer. Part of it she could attribute to being the oldest and always having to protect her younger sisters. But she knew a bigger factor was that she liked working on someone else's problems because it made it easier to ignore her own.

She knew that there had to be something more going on in her psyche. How else could she explain that the first man she'd been interested in since her husband's death was the one man she knew there was no chance of forever with?

They might have had fun tonight, and the sex had blown her mind, but she didn't kid herself that it would ever be more than a short-term affair. She guessed a part of her felt like justifying it by saying he was broken. Because he'd never known love. That was so much easier than admitting that she was broken, too.

He put his clothes on the padded bench at the end of the bed and then slid into bed next to her. He punched the pillows on his side of the bed and moved around before settling down. The television still played quietly in the corner.

He turned his head on the pillow to face her. She was lying next to him in what she thought of as the death pose: feet crossed at the ankles and her hands folded together over her stomach.

"Mind if I put on SportsCenter?" he asked.

Just like that, the tension she'd felt disappeared. Maybe she was reading too much emotion into the situation because she was a girl. But he was a guy. And nothing made her feel more normal than his request to watch sports.

"Sure."

He grabbed the remote, fiddled with the channels and then put it back down once he'd found his station. Then he lifted his arm and looked over at her. "Cuddle?"

It was the last thing she'd expected from him and she hesitated for a second. Hugging him in her bed in the middle of the night seemed more of an emotional risk than sex had.

But she had slept alone snuggled up with a pillow for too many nights to resist his tempting offer. He'd never have to know how much she needed this. As she slid down next to him, putting her head on his shoulder and wrapping one arm over his stomach, she felt surrounded by his warmth and the scent of his aftershave. Tears burned the back of her eyes as she was forced to confront the fact that she wanted this to be real. Wanted this to be forever. Wanted him to stay in her bed and hold her for the rest of her nights.

She knew it had nothing to do with love. It was motivated by loneliness, which made her face the truth behind why she'd been so willing to invite him to spend the night in the first place. Admitting to herself that it could be motivated by the fact that she was single while her sisters were nicely paired up and finding a kind of happily ever after was hard.

But there it was.

"Settle down," he said.

"What?"

"I can practically hear you thinking," he said. "Let's just call this a one-off. For tonight you aren't a Chandler and I'm not a Montrose. We're not scarred by our pasts, we're just Emma and Kell and we wanted each other so we took a chance."

She nodded against his chest and he rubbed her back. She let her fears and worries slip away, and the first fingers of sleep wrapped themselves around her consciousness. She drifted off to the thought that denying the real world was a dumb thing to do.

But she had a solid night's sleep until the alarm went off and she woke to find Kell gone. He'd left a note on her nightstand saying he left early to avoid traffic. A decent excuse, and he'd saved her from having to explain to Mrs. Hawking about her overnight guest.

She turned off her alarm just as Sammy came running into her bedroom and jumped up on the bed.

"Morning!" he yelled before launching himself at her. She wrapped her arms around him and held him close, understanding for the first time that her life was never going to be easy or uncomplicated but she'd always have this sweet little guy by her side. They snuggled under the covers for ten minutes and talked about the fun things Sammy would do at day care today and how she had a big meeting at work. Sammy hugged her and said, "I love you." And then she put on *Arthur,* one of his favorite shows on PBS Kids, while she went and got ready for her day.

It felt like a normal morning. She was able to pretend that nothing extraordinary had happened right up until the moment she got in her Land Rover to head downtown to her meeting with the board. She felt a tingling in the pit of her stomach at the thought of seeing Kell again.

She knew his cousins and the rest of the board would be there and she had to be on her A game but she felt far away from that. She had changed. In twenty-four hours her entire world had shifted and suddenly she wondered if bowing out gracefully wasn't the only solution left to her.

"Where were you last night?" Allan asked as he entered Kell's office. His cousin had a grande Americano in one hand and a latte in the other. He handed the Americano to Kell and then sat down in the leather guest chair facing Kell's desk.

Allan draped his ankle over his knee as he sprawled in the chair. He looked different. It wasn't the clothing—he still dressed like a hipster accountant. But something was different. Then it hit Kell: Allan was content, relaxed…happy.

Not that his cousin had ever been truly miserable. As the son of Thomas Montrose's only daughter, Allan had been raised away from the bitterness of their grandfather and as far as Kell could tell had had a fairly normal upbringing. Of course, losing his best friend, John McCoy, in a car accident less than six months ago had shaken Allan. It had also brought him closer to Jessi Chandler—her best friend, Patti, had been married to John and died with him in the accident. The couple had left Allan and Jessi as guardians of their nine-month-old baby, Hannah. Now Allan and Jessi, who'd long hated each other's guts, were engaged.

"I had a dinner," Kell said. He didn't want to call it a date or mention Emma. He wasn't entirely sure what would happen next. He'd stayed last night, hadn't slept a wink as he'd held her. He'd felt how soundly she'd slept and realized how much the young widow must have missed having her husband by her side.

It didn't mean he was especially intuitive but he was certainly getting to know Emma better than he'd ever expected to.

"A dinner? Some kind of meeting?" Allan asked.

"Yeah. Why were you checking up on me?" Kell never did anything but business and in the spring and summer played beach volleyball in an amateur league. He supposed it would seem odd to Allan that he hadn't been home.

"Jessi had a book club thing last night and took Hannah with her so I stopped by your place to see if you wanted to hang out."

"Why not just call?" Kell asked. He knew that Allan hadn't tried his cell phone because he'd cleared his messages last night.

"Her book club was in your neighborhood," Allan said. "Just thought I'd drop by and see you. I haven't had a guys' night out in a while."

"And John's not around for you to talk to," Kell said gently, realizing his cousin was missing his friend. "I'm free tonight. Want to see if Dec is free? We can go to the Staples Center. The Lakers have a home game."

"I'll have to check with Jessi, but that sounds good," Allan said. "I do miss John. I can't tell you how many times I reach for the phone to just chat about Hannah or being with Jessi and a couple times I even dialed his old number."

Kell nodded and once again found himself wishing he knew the right way to react to this. He was sad that John had died. But his own father had died young and Kell had grown up realizing that fate was fickle in terms of those it chose to take. Kell knew his own life would have been so much better if his father had lived.

Hannah was luckier in that respect than he'd been. Jessi and Allan loved her and were providing a stable home for the orphaned baby. Kell had no idea if he could ever provide anything like that for anyone. Least of all Emma—not that they were anywhere close to that type of relationship.

Just once he wanted to be normal. To have the same things that everyone else did. The things that other men took for granted. Like the fact that they'd meet someone and fall in love and have a family.

These were things he could attempt to find but his life had been dominated by hate and a thirst for revenge for so long that he suspected he'd never be able to settle down into any sort of domesticity.

He rubbed the back of his neck and realized that Allan had been talking. Saying something that he no doubt would expect Kell to respond to.

"I'm sorry, what'd you say?"

"I asked who the Lakers were playing."

Kell had no idea. Playtone kept a box at the Staples Center. Most of the time they used it to entertain corporate clients but occasionally the Montrose brothers went there to kick back and enjoy a game.

"Not sure. I'll check while you text Dec."

"Okay," Allan said, pulling his phone out of his pocket. Kell was willing to bet the first text was to Jessi.

He surfed the net and found that the Lakers were playing the Dallas Mavericks. Allan had gotten up and walked to the hallway to talk on the phone. From the hushed sound of the conversation, Kell suspected he was talking to Jessi.

Since he had the internet up, he typed in Emma's deceased husband's name and did a Google search. A list of photos and articles about him popped up. He clicked on the first link and felt sick at Emma's loss. Helio had been a decent guy who'd loved his young wife and his jet-set lifestyle. Most of the articles called Emma a video game heiress. He recalled that she hadn't really been working full-time at Infinity Games until after Helio's death.

"Dec's in," Allan said, walking back in the rom.

Kell closed the window on this laptop and looked over at his cousin. "Great. They are playing the Mavs. So it should be interesting."

"Nice," Allan said. "I'll see you at ten for the meeting with Emma. She sent some updated figures just now. I'm going to plug them into the financial sheets so I have the most current projections for our meeting."

"Sounds good. See you at ten."

When his cousin left, Kell knew he should be checking his email and analyzing the information Emma had sent but instead he surfed the net and realized that he was never going to be the right guy for Emma. No amount of wishing or changing could make him into the kind of man she deserved.

Eight

"Sammy said you had Darth over for dinner last night," Jessi said, walking into Emma's office like the badass Goth chick she was. She stood there in the doorway, in combat boots and a short plaid skirt, her arms crossed over her chest. "What gives?"

"We…we have to try to make peace. I'm the only one without a place in the new world order," Emma said. No way was she getting into everything else that Kell brought to the surface in her. Like the way he'd held her all night. It had been the best night's sleep she'd had in months.

She refused to dwell on it or give him any of the credit. It had been a long time since she'd had sex and it had to be down to the physical exhaustion she'd felt.

"You don't have to have him to your house for dinner," Jessi pointed out. She walked into the office, closing the door behind her. "Talk to me, Ems."

"No."

"No? Then something happened between the two of you," Jessi said, arching both eyebrows at her. "I have a bet with Allan that you will never give in to Kell. Don't make me lose."

"I'm not worried about some dumb bet you made with your fiancé. Kell and I have history. More than you guys can ever understand."

"I'm worried about the bet," Jessi said. "What history?"

Emma fiddled with her pen cup, rearranging the neat Pilot pens in color order and then deciding they'd be better in her drawer. She didn't want to admit to Jessi that she'd seen their grandfather be a Grade A jackass to Kell but then her sister already knew the truth about their grandfather.

"We were interns together. Remember when grandfather had that open call for students interested in going into the gaming industry?"

Her sister nodded. "I ran as fast as I could in the opposite direction."

"You did, but ended up here nonetheless." Emma had always been a strong believer in fate. And it seemed that there was some higher power at work here at Playtone-Infinity Games as well. The long ago feud started by Gregory Chandler and Thomas Montrose was being settled by this generation. And not in a way either of the men would have approved of.

"I did. Gramps must be chuckling over that," Jessi said wryly.

Emma shook her head. "And rolling his eyes that you called him Gramps and then having a fit that we let Infinity Games fall into the hands of his hated rival."

"Definitely. So, back to Kell. He came here as an intern?" Jessie asked.

Emma nodded. She didn't really want to talk about Kell Montrose. The more she and Jessi discussed him the more uncomfortable Emma was. She knew that Kell would hate it if he ever heard them talking about him.

"He's more gutsy than I would have guessed. What was his play?"

Emma thought about it. Given what she knew of Kell, she suspected that Thomas Montrose might have been the reason why Kell came to work with them. That Kell had wanted to prove something to his grandfather and bring back some information on Infinity Games. "I think he wanted to learn gaming and check out his grandfather's enemy. Kell grew up with Thomas."

"Allan told me. He's pretty much the only one who wasn't screwed up by Thomas. Of course, he turned into an arrogant show-off instead."

"I thought you didn't call him names anymore," Emma said.

"Old habit. Plus I don't want him getting too complacent."

"Good plan. How's Hannah doing? Still teething?" Emma asked.

"Yes. We tried every over-the-counter remedy. And

then I talked to Patti's mom. She was having a very lucid day where she knew who I was and everything," Jessi said. "She suggested rubbing rum on Hannah's gums. I know, I know, it's not the accepted thing but we were desperate and tried it. Guess what? It worked."

Patti's mom suffered from Alzheimer's and most days lived in a the very distant past when Patti and Jessi were teens, so often when Jessi talked to her it was a struggle.

Emma admired her sister for not only taking on raising Patti's daughter but also caring for her mother. Patti had been so much more than a friend to Jessi and Emma knew her sister still struggled with the loss.

"Speak of the devil," Jessi said.

"Allan, Kell or the actual devil?"

"Haha. Allan. He wants to hang out with his cousins tonight. What do you say to a girls' night? I've missed hanging out with you and Cari. There isn't enough time to see everyone," Jessi said.

"Sounds great to me. I'll get Mrs. Hawking to stay late and watch our kids so we can go out."

"Love it. I can't believe we all have kids. I was never going to have them," Jessi said.

"I always thought you were just saying that to make Dad mad."

"Partially. But I also saw how screwed up he was and how hard it was for me to fit in at home and just never wanted to put another person through that."

"You turned out okay," Emma said.

"Thanks to my big sis," Jessi said. "You sure you're okay with the Kell thing?"

"Yes," Emma said. "On another subject I've got the meeting with the board this morning. Did your team finish the mock-ups of the game so we can use it in the demo?"

"Yes. And I did go talk to the kids in the childcare area yesterday. So I have some initial focus group feedback for you, too."

They discussed the results and made a few tweaks to the reading app prototype. When Jessi left, Emma sat back in her chair and contemplated how fate might have a different plan for her than the one she had seen in her future just a few days ago. A plan that involved Kell Montrose more than ever. The only problem with that plan was she had no real idea of how Kell would react.

The boardroom at Playtone-Infinity Games didn't have that old world boys' club feel to it. It was hip and young. At one end of the conference room, there was an Xbox One connected to a huge forty-inch flat screen television. The latest PlayStation was at the other end, and the common area outside the boardroom featured the Wii. The company developed games across all the platforms; they were mainly known for their first-person shooters, massively multiplayer online games that had gamers from all over the world competing against each other.

Kell sat at the head of the table thinking about how long and hard the road to get here had been. But it was so worth it. It hadn't only been about the vengeance. They'd had true success in their industry. When he sat here surrounded by the awards they'd garnered and the corporate portraits of his cousins and him hanging on the wall, he felt a sense of satisfaction knowing he'd done what his grandfather hadn't been able to.

But that feeling faded as Emma walked into the room. She wore a wide-legged pantsuit with a fitted jacket and a jewel-toned shirt, and her hair was pulled back in a conservative style. When she noticed him, she gave him a forced smile.

"I was hoping to get here early to set up," she said as she put a large portfolio on the table and set her big leather bag on one of the chairs.

All business. But then he shouldn't have expected anything else. She wasn't going to suddenly want to talk about last night. He hoped his note was enough. And he was torn. A part of him knew one night in her arms wasn't enough but another part wasn't sure it was wise to ever go back again.

"Do you need my help?"

"Sure. I've got some foam core boards in the portfolio. Would you put them up on the credenza while I get out the tablets and cue up our prototype?"

"I'd be happy to," he said, getting up and walking over to her. Her perfume surrounded him and he closed his eyes as memories of the night before assailed him.

He turned away to get his body back under control and then took the portfolio and began setting up her boards. If he'd needed proof that last night had been a mistake then he had it. There was no clearer evidence than the fact that he was still obsessing over her. He had the feeling he always would be. There was something about Emma that affected him that deeply.

He shook his head and focused on the task at hand. As he looked over the boards, he had to admit she'd really made a lot of progress from their initial chat about her future with Playtone-Infinity Games. He was impressed but knew he shouldn't be. He'd always thought of her as a worthy adversary and her work here proved that maybe if she'd been given enough time she might have been able to turn Infinity Games around. Then again, that had never been an option, given that he'd been gunning for her.

She sat at the end of the table near the door with a small pile of tablets next to her. She was setting up something on each device. He knew that Allan was going to have the financials for them all to review. Once they had a product they could decide if they should have a for-profit educational arm or if they'd release the games through a non-profit foundation as Emma had originally suggested.

"Why are you staring at me?" she asked without looking up.

"Just marveling over how much you've done in such a short time," he said.

She glanced up at him with a cynical look. "I know you didn't expect it."

"You're right, I didn't. And that was my mistake. I think I underestimated you, Emma."

"You were blinded by your thirst for Chandler blood."

"I've certainly changed my focus."

"Have you?"

"I think so," he said. But he wasn't a hundred percent sure. It was easy right now when everything was going well to say he'd given up his quest for vengeance but it had been a part of him for so long that he felt it'd be stupid to assume it was all gone.

"Not sure?" she asked. "Me either."

"It's complicated."

She nodded. "I said as much to Jessi earlier when she asked me why I had you over to dinner at my house last night."

"You did? How did she find out about that?"

"Sammy mentioned that Darth had paid us a visit," Emma said with a rue smile. "Sammy doesn't know it's not a nice name."

"It's growing on me," Kell said, but the truth was he didn't want Emma or her son to think of him as the bad guy. Hell. He wanted something different now but still wasn't sure if he could pull it off. He knew he had to let go of the past; he'd won the battle over Infinity Games so there was no reason to keep living with the resentments that had motivated him. But he wasn't sure how to move forward.

Sex with Emma had been great, but he wasn't sure that was the way forward either, because sleeping with her had made his life even more complicated than before. Still, he wanted her, now that he knew just how hot her kisses made him. And how perfect she tasted and how right she felt in his arms.

But he wasn't the right kind of guy to hold a woman in his arms forever. He hoped she realized that because he didn't want to hurt her. She'd had enough of that in her romantic life. She needed a white knight. A hero. A man who wasn't broken.

Emma made her presentation to the Playtone-Infinity Games board then answered their questions. She'd put in the hard work so she was ready for the tough topics they brought up.

"I know you mentioned doing this as a charitable foundation," Kell said. "Have you considered possibly using this first game to launch a for-profit educational division?"

"I hadn't considered that. I just tried to find a place in the merged company where my leadership skills were needed. The foundation model was the first thing that came to mind."

"And I appreciate that," Kell said. "But based on the focus group feedback—thanks for that—Jessi—I think we should look at the numbers if we opened a new division. It could be based out of the Malibu campus, which we were talking about selling off."

"You were going to sell it off?" Cari asked. "Why wasn't I notified?"

"We don't need two offices with two staffs," Dec said. "You knew that the five year plan had closures in it."

"Did I?" Cari asked. "I don't remember that being mentioned, but I like the idea of using Infinity's old offices for an education division. I think that market is exploding and we could be on the cusp of capturing a huge audience."

"I agree," Allan said. "The numbers I ran were

based on setting everything up as a nonprofit. But I can easily come up with a new set of projections. We're going to need more information and a fully developed demo before I can commit money."

"Okay. Seems like we should meet back here in three weeks. Emma, get a working game and some video of the game being tested by our target audience. Jessi, maybe set up a focus group with parents to get their feedback as well. We know what kids want but we need to ensure parents will buy it," Kell said.

Emma felt better than she'd expected to. She marked the date in her planner. She knew in the digital age she should be putting it in her phone but she preferred pen and paper.

When the meeting was over, everyone gathered their things and left except Kell. She was surprised when he got up and gathered her boards.

"I want to be hands-on with this project. I'm going to rearrange my schedule so I can be at your office on Friday to spend some time with the kids."

She nodded. He was the boss but she felt as if he didn't trust her to do her job. "But I can take it from here if you're busy."

"I know. But I'm used to being involved with everything that we develop. I don't think I could step back now."

"Fine. If that's what you want," she said, shoving the tablets in her bag and trying not to feel as if she'd been sent to the principal's office. But that was hard. She knew that he was in charge. He'd made that quite clear. But she didn't like micromanagers. She was grateful to still have her job, but she thought he'd come to trust her at least a little bit.

"It is," he said arrogantly.

"Why are you being so jerky about this?" she asked.

"Am I? I'm not going to just let you go off and spend money unsupervised, Emma. It's my company no matter what happens between us—"

She stood up and walked over to him. "I know I'm still on probation and the same conditions are still in place. You don't have to prove yourself on that score."

She put her hand on his back but he flinched. "It's not you who I was proving myself to."

"Then who? Our family has no idea that anything has happened between us," she said. And if she had her way, they never would.

He turned away and she let her hand drop to her side as he leaned in close, staring at her with those intense eyes of his. "Myself. I want to believe I still have my edge and you haven't dulled it."

"You do," she said. She knew he'd never let any woman, especially one who'd been born a Chandler, have that much influence over him.

"Really?" he asked, taking her hand in his and bringing it to his chest. He held her hand there and she felt the beat of his heart grow more rapid.

"Feel that?" he asked. "I'm totally pretending you have no effect on me, but it's not true. I need to keep my perspective. I don't want to fall prey to some kind of silly emotion."

"Silly emotion? Like what? This is lust." She stepped closer and put her other hand on his shoulder.

"We want each other and that is the only thing between us right now."

"Are you sure of that?" he asked. "Last night it felt like more and I know it did to you as well."

"How do you know that?" she demanded. "Can you read minds now?"

"I don't have to. I can read your face, Emma, and you were scared last night. Afraid of the implications of what we'd done, the same as I was. Both of us are scrambling to find normal again and if that means I have to micromanage you to feel like things are the way they should be, then that is what I'm going to do."

"You're the boss," she said, rising on tiptoe and biting him on the earlobe. She heard his sucked-in breath and felt his heartbeat race. "But that seems like the dumbest idea in the world. The more time we spend together the more we are going to want to rip each other's clothes off."

She picked up her bag and walked out of the boardroom.

Nine

Kell pulled into the parking lot at the Staples Center wearing his Steven Nash jersey. He was a longtime fan and had been happy when Nash had transferred to L.A. to play out the end of his career.

As Kell walked into the arena, he noticed that he'd received a text. He glanced down at his phone and saw that it was from Dec.

Little hiccup. We couldn't get a sitter for tonight so I am bringing DJ and Sammy. Allan is bringing Hannah.

What? This wasn't what he needed tonight. He kept trying to just get his life back to normal and now it was babies and cousins. He should just pretend he had a meeting and head back home. Except he didn't want to spend the night at home, alone and thinking about Emma, which is exactly what would happen.

He texted back. Fine.

Sorry. Being a dad is complicated.

I'm being a jerk. Sorry. I ordered our regular food for the box. Do I need anything extra for the babies?

Nah. I'll bring it. I'll be there in ten minutes or so. See ya then.

He entered their box and remembered the good old days when Dec would have brought girls with him instead of babies. God, life had changed a lot this past year. Of course, Kell had indirectly been the catalyst for that change so he shouldn't complain, but nothing had gone to his plan.

"Hiya," Allan said as he walked into the corporate box with a flowery diaper bag over one shoulder and baby Hannah in his arms. She wore a pair of purple leggings and what looked like a brand new Lakers T-shirt. She had her fist in her mouth and drool was dripping down her arm.

"Hello," Kell said. "Need a hand?"

"Yes. Miss Squirmy has been trying to get down since we entered the arena. You should have seen her in the store when we were buying her T-shirt. Luckily one of the sales girls helped me out," Allan said, handing Hannah to Kell.

Not exactly what he'd had in mind but he looked down at the little girl and she pulled her fist from her mouth and smiled at him. He smiled back and tried to hold on to the wriggling nine-month-old. But it was clear she wanted to be on her own to explore the room.

"Okay to let her loose?" he asked Allan.

"I think so."

He walked over to the bar, where the catering staff had laid out food and drinks and grabbed a napkin to dry Hannah's hand before he set her down. When he did, she took off like a rocket, crawling around the room. Kell had a chuckle, as he watched Allan following her.

His cousin was a changed man.

"I guess Dec got in touch with you," Allan said.

"Yes. It's not what I had planned but then life is different now, isn't it?"

"It sure is. I had no idea one little person could command so much of my time and energy. Jessi had mentioned bringing the baby with her but she said the girls needed some time to relax and talk. They are worried about Emma."

"What about?" Kell asked. He really didn't want their families to know that they had slept together. He got that women liked to talk about things but he wasn't looking forward to having a chat on the subject with his cousins. He'd given them both hell when they'd hooked up with other Chandler sisters.

The door opened and Dec walked in holding Sammy's hand and wearing a baby carrier on his chest with his eighteen-month-old son DJ in it. DJ was swinging his legs and had on a pair of sunglasses.

"I need a cold one," Dec said.

Kell shook his head as Sammy let go of Dec's hand and walked into the room. The toddler was dressed in a pair of jeans, Converse tennis shoes and a racecar T-shirt. He waved at Kell and walked over to him while Dec got DJ out of the carrier.

"Darth!"

"Dude, I wish you'd call me Kell."

"I like Darth," Sammy said.

Of course he did. "You like basketball?"

"I don't know," Sammy said.

Kell glanced around at his cousins with their babies and realized whether he wanted it or not, he and Sammy were going to be paired up tonight. Kell tried to show Sammy the court but the little guy couldn't see over the railing.

"Want me to pick you up?"

Sammy nodded and lifted his arms up toward him. Kell lifted him somewhat awkwardly, but Sammy knew how to be held and Kell caught on quickly. He pointed out the nets and talked a little about the game but then realized he was probably talking over the three-year-old's head.

"Hungry?"

Sammy nodded, and Kell carried him over to the bar and helped him make a plate of nachos with nothing spicy on it and then got him settled in a chair where he could see the game just in time for tip-off.

Sammy got into the game, standing and cheering whenever Kell, Allan and Dec did. Hannah fell asleep in Allan's arms by halftime and he left so that it was just Dec and DJ keeping Kell and Sammy company.

DJ and Sammy played on the floor with toy racecars that Dec had brought in DJ's bag. Kell and his cousin sat back, drinking Coke and enjoying the game as the boys played. The situation was so foreign to his life that Kell felt as if he was watching someone else. Even as a child he didn't have a lot of memories like this. Sometimes Dec, Allan and he would get together and hang out, but since there had been so much animosity in the family they had all been pretty much on their own.

"So, you're doing good with Sammy," Dec said in a leading way during a time-out in the game. It wasn't like his cousin to beat around the bush.

"Yeah. I had dinner with Emma last night. And I've been talking to Sam to get an idea about how he'd use the game she wants to develop."

"This seems like more than just market research," Dec said.

"Well, it's not," Kell said. He wasn't ready to be a stepfather to Emma's son. He wasn't even sure he was going to sleep with her again. He didn't want Dec speculating about him.

Dec just raised his eyebrows. "Whatever you say."

"I'm being an ass again, aren't I?"

"Yeah, but I know it's just because I cut a little too close to the truth."

"You did. Remember how I acted when you told us about Cari?" Kell asked.

"I try not to because you were a total jerk but yeah, I remember," Dec said.

"I'm that way toward myself," Kell said after a few minutes had passed. He was torn between being fascinated and experiencing something new that he'd never felt before and knowing that Emma was a Chandler and therefore off-limits. He was even conflicted over Sammy—by the fact that Gregory Chandler, the big, bad wolf from Kell's childhood, was the toddler's great-grandfather.

Dec reached over, clapping him on the shoulder. "It sounds like you might be falling for her."

"I'm not. It's just some sort of attraction based on proximity," Kell said.

"Never say that in front of a woman unless you want her to rip you a new one," Dec said.

"I wouldn't. I'm not talking to a woman unless all the baby care has turned you into one," Kell said. "Listen, I know it sounds ridiculous, but it really is the only explanation I've got right now. It makes sense to me that after you and Allan paired up with her sisters that we'd start to feel attracted to one another."

Dec nodded. "So what you're saying is that if we weren't involved with her sisters you wouldn't even notice Emma?"

He nodded at his cousin, and then luckily the game resumed before Kell was forced to admit he'd become a big liar. Even before his cousins had met Jessi and Cari, Kell had been attracted to Emma.

DJ and Sammy came back over to them and Dec scooped his son up, holding him on his lap as the game got underway. Sammy stood there looking around and then walked over to Kell and just stared at him.

Kell saw himself in that little toddler. Remembered what it felt like to be the only kid at school without a dad on those days when parents were invited to the classroom. He didn't care what happened with Emma; he knew he had to be careful not to harm Sam. Not just for the boy's sake but also for his own.

He reached down and scooped the three-year-old up. Sammy didn't say anything; he just settled down on Kell's lap and put his arm around him, resting his head against Kell's chest.

Kell sat there as emotions—real emotions he couldn't deny—stirred in him. He wanted to be the kind of man who would be a good father to Sammy. He knew that Emma deserved a man who would do that for her.

But for a brief instant he wished that he could be that man. He knew that it was a stretch and never in his life had family or forever been a part of the picture, but tonight he sort of wished it was.

Emma had had a moment's panic when she realized that Dec and Allan were going to be watching all the babies and hanging out with Kell. Mrs. Hawking's granddaughter had the lead role in a play at her school so Mrs. Hawking needed the night off. It wasn't his normal situation and she didn't know if he'd be able to handle it. But then she reminded herself that she wasn't responsible for him or his happiness. She trusted her soon-to-be brothers-in-law with her son.

The Chandler sisters had decided to go to a night-club on the beach near their homes. It had been a long time since they'd all been to a club together. At least since before the merger, if not before Emma had met Helio. Her life had been going on fast-forward for the last five years. She felt as if she'd lost herself somewhere in that race.

And she no longer knew who she was. She had taken to defining herself as a mom. Being Sammy's mom took a lot of her time and it was easy to see herself only in that role. But the other night with Kell she'd been reminded that she was still a young woman with needs, desires and dreams for her future that hadn't died with Helio or the loss of Infinity Games. Those two things were tied together in her head and always would be. Infinity Games had saved her sanity when she'd been widowed. She'd needed it, and maybe that was why she was spinning her wheels now about Kell.

She knew that she didn't need the company the way she used to, but until the board had delivered that ultimatum to her she had been ignoring the fact that her future was her own again. She hadn't meant to lose Infinity Games, but having done so she realized it freed her up.

She sighed without meaning to as a sense of relief surged through her when they all took a seat at the cocktail table.

"You okay?" Cari asked.

"Yes," Emma said, and for the first time in a long time she realized she truly was okay. She knew that whatever happened with Kell she was going to embrace it. And see where it led. She was tired of sitting in the backseat and watching life pass her by.

"Good. You seemed a little off today," Cari said.

"It was a tiny bit stressful to be presenting an idea to the board and knowing the stakes were high if I screwed it up. I always feel like Grandfather is watching me, ready to pounce if I haven't thought of every detail."

It was true. The fact that she'd been remembering how Kell looked naked standing in her bedroom had also been distracting, but she didn't want to mention that to her sisters.

"Gramps was some piece of work. No wonder Dad was such a tyrant," Jessi said as she came back to their table in the corner with a round of pomegranate martinis.

"He was. I get why Mr. Montrose would hate us. You'd think Grandfather would have been happier having won the initial battle between them, but he didn't seem to ever be."

Cari took a sip of her drink and then shrugged. "I always thought he must have been embarrassed when he cut the Montroses out of the company. I mean, it had to be something that didn't sit right in his soul, you know?"

Emma wanted to smile at the sweet and caring spin that Cari put on their grandfather's ruthlessness. Her sister saw the world through her own rose-colored glasses and because she would never be able to do something like their grandfather had and live with it, she'd painted him in the same colors. But a part of Emma believed her grandfather was simply one of those people who were never happy. Who didn't like other people and therefore didn't feel guilty about the Montrose affair, but simply saw it as more collateral damage.

"Maybe. It doesn't matter. He's dead and the Montrose heirs have gotten their revenge.... They've sort of evened out the scales and now we're all in a better place," Jessi said. "Or we will be once we get Emma sorted out. I really didn't think I'd want to work for the merged company at first, but it just feels right now."

"It feels right because you're in love with a Montrose and you were instrumental in getting the merged company a big money contract with a Hollywood producer. I think we need to toast that again," Emma said. "To Jessi."

Cari and Jessi both lifted their glasses, clinking them against Emma's, and then all three sisters took a sip of their drinks. They ordered snacks and as the evening went on Emma tried to make peace with the jealousy she felt toward her sisters and their neat and tidy lives. She knew they'd both suffered a lot to get to the happy place they were in now.

"What's the matter, Emma?" Cari asked as she noticed her expression.

"Nothing," Emma said. No way was she going to cry on her sisters' shoulders and tell them that she wanted what they had. Or that she might want it with Kell. She knew enough about human psychology to realize that ever since she'd had sex with Kell, her hormones were trying to tell her he'd make the perfect mate.

"Liar," Jessi said. "Does this have anything to do with Kell?"

Emma shook her head. It had everything to do with Kell.

"What about Kell?" Cari asked.

"They had dinner together last night," Jessi said. "I suspect more than dinner."

"Ugh. Leave it be, please," Emma said.

"Did you when we asked you to leave us alone over Allan and Dec?" Jessi asked. "No, you had to go all big sister and try to give us advice and help us out."

Cari reached over and patted Emma's hand. "I hated that interference but knowing you had my back made everything easier. Tell us what's going on."

"Nothing at all, except that I might be losing it," Emma said.

"How?"

"I'm attracted to Kell."

"He's not bad looking," Jessi said.

"Jess!"

"What? He's like I imagine Lucifer looks. With those dreamy silver eyes and those curls. Who has curls anymore? He should look ridiculous but he doesn't," Jessi said.

Cari laughed. "You have a point. He does have a sort of fallen angel look about him."

"You guys aren't helping. I think it's just lust or something. Maybe—and I'm not at all happy with myself for feeling this way—but maybe it's motivated by envy."

"Of us?" Jessi asked.

Emma nodded.

"Yes! Finally all my childhood wishes that someday you'd want something I had have come true. I thought they never would," Jessi crowed.

Emma shook her head at her sister. "Grow up. I didn't say I was envious, just that I think I feel left out. Helio's dead. Sure, I have Sammy—I'm not necessarily saying something is missing in my life. But when Kell and I kissed, it awakened something I'd forgotten was part of me."

"What?"

"A longing for something that I can't have."

"Why can't you have it?" Cari asked. "I think you'd make a lovely couple."

Jessi snorted.

"Nice try. But we both know that revenge has been a part of Kell's DNA for so long that there is no way he will ever be able to be with me and let himself be happy. I'm still the enemy."

"Are you saying you love him?" Jessi asked.

"No. Not at all. Just that there are moments when I think if our grandfathers hadn't been intent on screwing each other over...well, maybe Kell and I would have had a chance."

Cari shook her head. "This makes me so mad. You'd think decisions made decades before we were born wouldn't affect our lives but we are living with the consequences."

"I know," Emma said.

"What are you going to do?" Jessi asked. "And don't say ignore it. Lust is powerful and you two are spending a lot of time together. It'll be like when Allan and I were trapped during that hurricane on the Outer Banks."

Jessi and Allan had been in North Carolina after the deaths of the best friends. They had been named co-guardians to their friends' daughter, Hannah, and it had taken weeks for the judge to grant them guardianship. While they were waiting, they'd had to survive a hurricane. Somehow during that intense time the two rivals had fallen for each other.

"I don't know," Emma said. "I'm thinking of walking away from the company and taking Sammy on a vacation to Spain. His *abuela* has been begging me to come for a visit. It would be a nice escape."

"Really?" Jessi asked. "I like Helio's mom but she'd see that you were running away."

"She would let me. I was strong when she needed me to be. She said when I needed her she'd be there for me," Emma said. The thought of going to Madrid and living in the beautiful Moorish house that Isabella owned was tempting. Her former mother-in-law would pamper her and watch over Sammy, and Emma could pretend that she had no problems.

But running away had never been her style and she wasn't about to start now. Or at least that was what she told herself. But inside she knew she was staying because she wanted to see what would happen next with Kell Montrose.

Ten

Kell felt like Mr. Creeper parking in front of Emma's house just after midnight but he hadn't been able to sleep. He wanted something that he didn't know how to get. Something that was inexplicably tied to her. And now he was losing sleep over it.

After Dec had taken Sammy and left the Lakers game, Kell had gone home alone. His posh downtown condo hadn't felt welcoming at all. The bedroom was too quiet and he was reminded he was alone. He knew it was his own choice to be that way but he'd been unable to reconcile the life he had with the glimpse of the life he wanted.

And he did want something more. But as usual he was afraid to name it. It had been so long since he'd thought of family as anything other than a solid motivation for the business decisions he made.

But his idea of family now involved something emotional and needy. *Hell. Just...hell.* He should have called. Or not called. This was crazy. But here he was in Malibu and he'd never been a coward and he wasn't going to start being one now.

He took out his cell phone and texted Emma. Can we talk?

After a couple minutes, he received a response. Now?

Yes. I'm outside your house.

Seriously?

Totally. I'll understand if you don't want to.

It's fine. Give me a few minutes and I'll come to the door.

He felt a pang in his heart.
Forget it.
No way. Two minutes tops.
He got out of his car, hit the button for the auto locks and walked up to her house. He shivered in the mid-January chill and shoved his hands into his pockets as he moved. The front walk was lit with those little solar-powered path lights. When he got to the front door and was waiting for Emma to come and open it, he glanced to his left and saw a stepping stone with two

little handprints and Sam's name on it. He went back down the porch steps to look at it more closely.

She had her own life. Why was he here? He couldn't say he wanted to be part of it unless he could really give it a go. And that was what scared him the most. He wanted this with the kind of keen longing that made him shake when he dwelled on it. He also knew himself well enough to understand that the things he wanted the most were the ones that made him act like an idiot.

The door opened and the warm glow of the hall light spilled onto her front porch. He was down there just out of the cone of light, hiding in the dark like Quasimodo in his bell tower. Maybe he should stay in the shadows and just enjoy observing her life from a distance.

Then again, it looked as if he was going to have Emma in his life whether they were romantically involved or not. They worked together. They were connected by marriage and extended familial bonds. Was that enough?

No. Hell, no. It wasn't enough. Why couldn't he have his shot at a life in the light? He'd done what he needed to. Fulfilled his obligation as the eldest cousin. Satisfied the family vendetta.

"Kell?"

"I'm here. Just having second thoughts."

"Given that it's two a.m. I sort of get that. But why don't you come inside," she suggested.

He glanced up and saw her standing in the doorway in a light green bathrobe that ended mid-thigh. Her hair was tousled and fell in soft waves around her shoulders

And her eyes were sleepy. She held one hand against her chest while she waited for his answer.

The keen need sliced through him again and he admitted it wasn't just family that he wanted to be a part of. He wanted to be her lover. To be part of a couple. To have someone.

"I...."

For the first time, he had no idea how to act or what to do next. What he wanted were things he didn't know how to take and wasn't even sure he had the right to.

Still illuminated by that cone of light, she left the doorway and walked down the steps. She took his hand in hers, linked their fingers together and led him inside. He followed her because it was all he desired.

Once in her foyer she closed the front door, dropped his hand and went to reset the alarm on a keypad near the door.

"Hot cocoa?"

"Sure," he said as the warmth of her house seeped into his clothes. But the thing that warmed him to the bone was the easy way she led him to the kitchen as if it weren't the middle of the night.

As if he somehow belonged here. It hit him that this was what he had always wanted and never really been able to find. Belonging. A place to call his own.

But Emma wasn't his. Despite one night together. And he guessed that was why he'd come here tonight.

"Sit down and talk," she said. She moved around her kitchen getting milk from the fridge, a saucepan from under the sink and a bar of chocolate from the pantry.

"I'm waiting," she said, while he sat there at her breakfast bar watching her.

He shrugged out of his jacket and draped it over the back of his chair, and then leaned his elbows on the counter and tried to think where to start.

"Did Sammy tell you about the game?"

"He said it was fun. Thank you for buying him that basketball. He's sleeping with it in his bed," Emma said. "I hadn't realized how much he missed having a guy of his own. Dec and Allan are both good when they come over but Sammy is always very aware that they belong to DJ and Hannah."

There it was. Sammy needed him, too. But he had no idea if he could stay—not for a few nights or a few basketball games, but forever. That fear kept him from risking it. Wouldn't he be doing more damage if he tried and failed?

Emma had never seen Kell like this. He had on a pair of faded Levis, a Playtone Games T-shirt and stubble on his jaw. His hair was mussed as if he'd run his hands through it a number of times. She wanted to just go and wrap her arms around him the way she did with Sammy when he was scared.

But the thought of Kell having that kind of fear made no sense. He was intelligent and driven and always knew exactly what he wanted. Tonight he seemed different and she wondered why he was really here. The milk began to simmer and she took it off the heat and added the chocolate bar and then a smidge of vanilla. She stirred the hot chocolate as if it was her first time making it, instead of a recipe she knew by heart.

"I guess that's kind of why I'm here. I felt like Sammy when I was a kid. I didn't have someone of my own."

"Surely your grandfather went places with you," she said.

"Did your grandfather spend that much time with you?"

"No," she said. Her grandfather was a dedicated business professional and had no time for his granddaughters or their lives. Luckily, her grandmother and mother had been there for them. "Is that why you're here?"

He shoved his hands through his hair and stood up so quickly that he rocked the chair back on itself. He came over to her and leaned against the counter next to her. "Yes and no."

"I don't understand," she said. "I'm trying, but you're being too vague."

"I don't know how to say this, Emma. It's going to sound stupid and I abhor that but I can't think of another way. I saw Sam tonight and he reminded me of myself and then I thought about you, how much I still want you even though I thought one night would be enough. And then usually when I'm with Dec and Allan and their kids, I feel something empty inside of me. But I didn't feel that way tonight when I had Sam with me."

"Okay. So you want to try having a relationship?"

she asked. It would be complicated but she had to admit she wasn't entirely opposed to the idea.

"Yes and no."

"Again? I've never known you to be so indecisive."

He turned to her and she'd never seen such stark emotions on his face. There was longing and fear and a million other things there, the emotions so bare that it almost hurt to look at him. She put her hand on his arm.

"I don't know if it's just because everyone else has someone or if it's real between us, you know? And I don't want to take a chance and then screw it up for you and Sammy. You've both had your share of pain and I don't want to add to that."

His words hit home, and even though she knew that in the morning he might feel differently, she had to say the right thing now. So, of course her mind went blank and she felt the tingly feeling in her spine that she meant she was about to do something rash.

She was a mom. She had to think of how this would affect Sammy. But she was also a woman and what Kell was offering was something she wanted. *That's right,* her mind said, *you do want him.* And how would Sammy be affected if his mom never did anything because she was afraid to risk her heart?

"I don't want to be hurt either, but I guess we'll never know if we don't try, right?" she said after a few moments passed.

He arched one eyebrow at her. "That's one way of looking at it."

"It is. We can both just do what we can, you know?

If I see Sammy getting too attached to you and things aren't going well between us, I can pull the plug."

"Fair enough," he said. "What if you start getting too attached?"

He rested his arm on the counter behind her, almost crowding her with his closeness. She put her hand on his chest but she admitted to herself it wasn't to stop him. It was to touch him because she had been wanting to do that since the moment he'd texted her tonight.

"I'm not sure. I don't want to be stupid but you know how these things are," she said, remembering that headlong rush into her relationship with Helio. From the first moment she'd fallen for him she'd known it was stupid. He lived a dangerous life. Kell didn't take those risks with his physical person but he was just as dangerous to her.

She knew she'd said it before but it had never sunk in. It didn't matter to her that he was a man who'd been consumed by bitterness and revenge for most of his life. A part of her wanted to heal him and fix him. And every other part of her thought it didn't matter because she needed him. Now.

Tonight when she'd thought of giving up and running away to Spain it had become clear to her that the last thing she wanted was to leave until she knew what could be with Kell. She wasn't saying it was real or even love. And if he hadn't shown up tonight she might have been able to let it be, but here he was.

"What are you thinking?" he asked.

She lifted her hand, rubbing her finger against the stubble on his jaw and leaning in close because the truths that were the hardest to share could only be said in a whisper.

"I need you."

That was exactly what he needed to hear. He pulled her into his arms and buried his face in her neck. The embrace was one of comfort instead of lust at first, but he couldn't hold her this close and not react. He felt himself harden as she turned more fully into his arms and pressed herself to him. Then he lifted his head and found her mouth with his.

He kissed her deeply, leaving no doubt that he needed her as well. He picked her up and set her on the counter, and then stepped between her thighs. She wrapped her legs around his hips as he loosened the belt on her robe.

She wore a soft cotton pajama top with little pearl buttons down the front. He reached for them, fumbling with the tiny buttons, which felt too small for his hands. When she brushed him away and undid the buttons herself, he realized his hands were shaking.

Why did she get to him like this? Why was she the only woman who could make him feel this way? He realized he didn't have time for such questions as he pushed the nightshirt off her shoulders and leaned down to take one nipple in his mouth.

He couldn't go slow tonight, he needed her, needed this with such intensity that he felt his chest tighten as she put her hands on the back of his head, plunging her fingers into his hair.

He lightly bit her nipple as she arched back on the

counter. Then he lifted her up with one arm around her waist and pulled her panties off with his other hand. After tossing them on the floor, he leaned down to bury his face between her legs.

He was surrounded by her and then lifted his head to part her with his fingers. The full bud of her passion was revealed, and when he leaned down to tap it with his tongue, she moaned deep in her throat. Her hands came back to his shoulders as he moved in closer and continued to pleasure her with his tongue until her hips started to rise faster and faster against him and her thighs clenched around his head. When she reached the breaking point, she cried out his name.

He kept his mouth where it was, teasing out her orgasm for as long as he could. She fell forward against him and wrapped her arms around his shoulders. He was hard inside his jeans; it was a surprise he hadn't already come in them. She tugged at his T-shirt, pulling it up over his head and then leaned forward to nibble at his chest as her fingers teased a pattern down his abdomen and stomach to his waistband.

She undid his pants, reaching inside to stroke him through his underwear. His hips jerked forward; he needed her now. She held his naked flesh in her hand, and he fumbled in his pocket for the condom he'd put in there earlier.

He pulled it out, stepping back to push his underwear and pants out of the way before tearing open the packet, but she took it from him. She stroked his length up and down and then reached lower to cup him as she slowly slid the condom on. Then she tugged him forward, her grip firm on his erection.

He moaned as she brought him to her. Their eyes met as he thrust in with one long stroke, making her take him all. She moaned and shifted around, wrapping her legs around his hips as he lifted her off the counter and spun around so he could rest his back on it while she moved up and down on him.

He cupped her butt and felt her tighten around him until he knew he was on the edge and about to come. He lowered his head and tongued her nipple as she dug her fingernails into his shoulders and cried his name again as she tightened around him.

He thrust harder and quicker and felt his own release building inside him. After thrusting two more times, he collapsed against the counter, holding her to him with his grip on her backside.

She rested her head on his chest and each exhalation of her breath stirred the hair there and teased his nipple. He put his hand on the back of her head and rubbed it.

"I need you, too," he said.

She lifted her head, giving him a half smile. "I know."

He shook his head because already doubt was rushing in, telling him he'd made a huge mistake, but as he gently separated their bodies and lowered her to her feet it didn't feel like one. It felt as if something he was afraid to define and in that moment he made a decision that he sensed he'd regret later.

He was going to hold on for the ride of his life and if they crashed and burned, he'd deal with the fallout.

Because honestly, he felt as if he'd found the one thing he'd always been afraid to admit he'd been searching for. And it wasn't revenge for a long ago slight; it was home. It was the sense of belonging that he had only ever glimpsed when he was in Emma's company, with her arms wrapped around him.

They moved apart to gather their clothes but there was none of the awkwardness that had accompanied the first time they'd made love. He knew that this time there was no denying what was between them.

"I guess I should go," he said, when they'd both cleaned up.

"I want you to stay," she said.

Eleven

It had been two weeks since Kell's midnight visit to her house. He'd left the following morning just before Sammy had gotten up. Since then, they'd fallen into a pattern that had nothing to do with work and everything to do with figuring out their relationship. Kell came to dinner a couple nights a week and they cooked together and then had some family time.

It seemed as if he wanted the family time as much as she did. One night they all played with the remote control cars Kell had brought for Sammy, another night they rocked on "Guitar Hero." Then there was the time Kell played his ukulele while Sammy played the same tune on his tablet. They played lots of songs, including "They Can't Take That Away From Me." The sweet gesture had touched her deeply, making her feel as if she and Kell were building something that could last.

The feeling became especially strong after Sammy went to bed and they curled up on the patio or in front of the television together and talked about their days and then made love. The only wrinkle she could see was that Kell never talked of the future. And he was careful to let Sammy only get so close to him. He only let her get so close as well, now that she thought about it.

She realized that he was careful to not come to her house every night. In fact he had a pattern of two nights with them and then three nights away. Knowing Kell, that had to be significant. She wanted to believe they were building a relationship but the more she dwelled on it the less that seemed true. What it felt like to her was a cohabitation where Kell got to try out all the things he wished someone had done for him when he was a kid…with the added bonus of sex with her.

She sat at her desk in the Malibu office mulling it all over. It was almost time to go home. She hadn't heard from Kell today but she knew he had a big meeting with some Japanese investors who were interested in buying into Playtone-Infinity. There was no denying the merged company was a powerhouse of intellectual property and talent. She hated that she was out of the loop on the merger since she was still on probation. She was dying to know what was going on.

That kind of negotiation was really the kind of thing she'd always loved about being the CEO of Infinity Games. Which made her realize that just developing a new educational game wasn't going to be her future. The game was progressing wonderfully and Emma had no doubt that the board would approve it. But she couldn't see herself in some office job without the excitement that came from running the company.

It just wasn't what she was meant to do. She knew she was nearing the point where she had to finally make the hard decision. Stay or leave. Her heart said to stay but her mind pointed out that her affair with Kell would end. And when it did, she'd be working for her former lover, seeing him at family events. What a nightmare.

Why hadn't her common sense kicked in before this?

But she knew the answer. She liked him. Hell, she more than liked him; if she wasn't careful, she'd let herself fall in love with him. And falling in love with Kell Montrose—and admitting to it—was about the dumbest thing she could do.

She knew it but it didn't stop her heart from speeding up when she went down to the company day care center to pick up Sammy and found Kell waiting on the bench outside.

"Hello," he said, looking up at her.

"Hey. How was your day?"

"Long, actually, and if you weren't on probation I think I could use your opinion on the offer they made us," Kell said as he rubbed the back of his neck.

"Why should it matter? At the end of the day I'm still a shareholder and my interest in the company is to see it profitable."

"Yeah, that's what I told Allan and Dec but they pointed out that if it were any other Chandler, the thought wouldn't even occur to me to ask for advice."

Any other Chandler? What did that mean? Did his cousins know they were lovers? She'd been careful to keep it from her sisters.

"Uh…I don't know what to say to that."

"I know. Me neither. It's not like they know we have a relationship," Kell said.

"What are you doing down here?" she asked.

"I just arrived. I knew you'd be here to pick up Sam so I figured I wait for you," he said. "We need to talk tonight."

She nodded. She'd been sort of thinking the same thing all day. It would be too easy to let their current situation just continue. And she knew she was denying the fact that he wasn't going to stay forever. She knew that.

"Let me get Sammy and we can go. Do you want to come to my place?"

"I was hoping you'd ask one of your sisters to watch Sammy," he said.

"I'll try, but it would be better to give them a day's notice. They've been working all day, too, and have their own babies to worry about," Emma said. "Plus I told Sammy we were making tacos tonight."

"Well, I don't want you to break a promise," he said. "Our conversation can wait until tomorrow."

"Are you still coming over?" she asked.

She had a feeling that he was going to break up with her and if that was the case why not just do it.

What else could he need to speak to her alone about? And why did she feel so sad and angry all at once at the thought of it?

"I don't know," he said.

Kell was caught between his past life and his desire for the future. He wasn't ready to admit that the last two weeks with Sammy and Emma had been the best of his life but he knew they had been. They'd made him feel as if he belonged. As though he had a place to call his own. Only he knew it wasn't his place. It was theirs, and they'd invited him into it.

He couldn't keep playing his game of only seeing them for two days and then staying away for three. In his mind that kept the scales firmly tipped in his favor. In the direction of the life he'd always had and always known.

His meeting today had made him realize that no matter how much he wanted to talk things over with Emma he'd pretty much made up his mind to assign her a position where she'd be able to work for the company but not have any real influence over it. And he'd decided that long before he'd gotten to know her. But to change his mind now…well, it would mean he'd have to admit that he'd changed.

And change wasn't part of his make-up. He'd tried long-term relationships before and most of the time they ended amicably but this one couldn't. He knew he was enjoying the newness of having two people— a ready-made family—who wanted and needed him in their lives. But the novelty wouldn't last, and then what would he do?

He wasn't on the outside looking in anymore. Two nights ago when he'd tucked Sammy into bed, the little boy had hugged him tight and called him Darth Dada. Which had been like a punch to the gut. He wanted to be Darth Dada to Sammy and be a husband to Emma but he didn't know if he could. It was easy to say he'd stay and be her man but he had no idea if he'd bolt the first time things got tough.

Or if she'd even want him once he told her that Playtone-Infinity Games would keep her on, but not in a position of power.

She was looking at him, waiting for an answer about tonight, and he had none. There had been something about Emma from the beginning that had enabled her to render him speechless and that hadn't changed. Only now it was because of how he felt.

Emotions. Who'd have guessed he had them?

"What *do* you know?" she asked at last.

"That I want to come over. But we have to talk business and I don't want you to infer things and then be mad later," he said.

She grabbed his wrist and pulled him down the hall away from the nursery door, where parents were starting to come out with their kids.

"This thing between us has nothing to do with business. You promised me a fair shake and I'm reporting to the board, not just you. Whatever happens on that score is up to the board and you, what happens between us, well, that's down to me and you…I know it's hard to separate the two."

"You say that now but what if the decision doesn't go your way?" he asked. The Japanese company had been clear that they didn't want to see any infighting if they were going to make an investment in Playtone-Infinity. And Kell had pretty much decided that not taking the offer wouldn't be sound business.

But Dec and Allan had made arguments against it. They thought that if they took outside money they'd leave themselves open to interference. Which is why he could use Emma's input, but if he asked her for it and then slotted her into the position he had in mind—operational head of the new educational games unit, reporting to Cari, she'd feel betrayed.

But she couldn't report to him. That would be a conflict of interest. So it was Cari or nothing.

In a way it would have been so much better if he'd never gotten involved with her. Because the more he looked at their situation the more he became convinced that it couldn't last. And that the ending was going to be messy and hurt him more than he had anticipated.

For a man who was known for making astute decisions this one had dumb-ass written all over it. What had he been thinking? But he knew the answer: he hadn't been thinking at all. He'd gone with his gut and now he was paying the price.

"I don't know," she said, quietly. "But I do know that no matter what happens neither of us is going to get what we want."

She had a point.

The door to the nursery opened and Sammy popped his head out and looked down the hall. "There they are. Can I go?"

Emma turned to her son and smiled at him. "Let me go and sign you out, Sammy. Sorry, we were busy talking."

"That's all right," Sammy said. Emma returned to the nursery, gave her son a hug and went inside for a moment. When she came back out and the two of them turned to walk away, Sammy reached back for Kell.

Kell hesitated but he couldn't resist the chance to be included and took the little boy's hand. Emma looked over at him. He saw her heart in her eyes and he knew it was past time for him to end this. They were already beyond the point of no return and unless he could commit himself to her—and he didn't want to take a chance on doing that—he owed it to her to leave now and cause as little damage as possible.

But not tonight, he thought as Sammy started talking to him in his toddler speak with those shortened words that he wouldn't have understood just a few weeks ago but now made perfect sense. He wanted to try play Mario Kart online tonight. Todd, Sammy's friend from day care, played it online with his dad. Apparently, Sam had told Todd that they'd all play against each other, with Kell on Sammy's team.

Kell agreed but he knew that this would be the last night they all had together. He couldn't keep filling a role in Emma's and Sam's lives that should be filled by a better man. A man who could stay and love them both.

Not a man like himself who was hollow inside.

* * *

Kell followed her home, pulling into the driveway behind her. As she turned off the ignition in her car, Sammy said, "I like Darth Dada."

"He's not your daddy," she said softly.

"I know. He's in heaven, but Darth is nice and he plays games with me. I think he could be a daddy."

Emma's heart broke. She knew Sam needed a dad. He hadn't missed having one until DJ got one and then Hannah arrived, and she immediately had two parents in Jessi and Allan. Sammy was the only one with no dad.

"He is nice but he's just a friend of ours. Let's not count on him to be a part of our family."

"Why not?"

"He's not used to family," Emma said. How could she explain something she barely understood to her son?

"Maybe we could show him," Sammy said.

She was saved from having to answer because just then Kell arrived at the passenger-side door and opened it.

"How was the ride?"

"Good," Sammy said. "Wanna play racing when we get inside?"

"I'd like that," Kell said. "Online, right? What time did you tell Todd we'd be on?"

"When we got home," he said to Kell.

He got Sam out of his car seat and put him down. When Emma came around from her side of the vehicle, her little boy looked up at her.

"See?" Sammy said. He was still desperately trying to make his point that Kell could be his daddy.

"Yes," she said. She could see how to a three-year-old, Kell's wanting to play games with him and eat dinner with them on a regular basis would be enough to make him part of their family.

But Emma knew better.

Emma went upstairs to get changed and sent Mrs. Hawking on her way, while Sammy and Kell went to the living room and fired up "Mario Kart" a racing game that they liked to play.

When she came back downstairs to make dinner, Emma began to feel as if her anxiety was getting the better of her. She knew what she'd seen in Kell's eyes earlier, and for the life her, though she couldn't figure out why, it seemed as if Kell was still planning to fire her.

She knew the demands of her probation were strict but she had been careful to fulfill them all. And she would have thought that after all the time they spent together he'd have softened in his attitude. But clearly that wasn't the case.

As much as she wanted to get mad at him because of that, she knew she couldn't because she'd made a big deal about keeping their work and personal lives separate.

So did that mean he was breaking the affair off, too, or was it just work? And would she really want to keep seeing him if he fired her? This was a nightmare. Why had she ever allowed him into her life?

As if she could have kept him out. As soon as they'd

kissed she'd been a goner. She'd wanted him in her house and in her neat little life as if he was the answer to what was missing instead of just a really good lay. From the beginning, she couldn't think in terms of the two of them simply having a sexual connection. It had always been more to her.

Still was. She listened to Sammy and Kell talking and laughing as they played "Mario Kart" in the other room and she smiled to herself before remembering that after tonight everything would change. She peaked into the living room, seeing them both sitting on the floor in front of the couch with a pile of pillows behind their backs.

Kell put his hands over Sammy's to show him how to do something on his game controller and Sammy looked up at him with adoration in his eyes. He needed a father. He wanted it to be Kell. Emma turned away. She had no idea what to do.

No matter what Kell wanted to talk to her about— either their relationship or her employment future— it wasn't going to be a happy conversation. His body language had already warned her.

She had the chicken sizzling in the wok and was busy slicing tomatoes when she realized that she'd stay with Kell even if he fired her. The thought startled her enough that the knife slipped and she sliced her finger. She dropped the knife and stared at the small cut as it started to sting and bleed.

Her mind was on autopilot as she grabbed a kitchen towel to blot the wound. Instead of thinking about what she was doing, she was coming to a realization about

Kell. She finally admitted to herself why her job didn't matter to her anymore: it was because she had fallen for him.

Lately, she was so happy when he called or texted her. Felt that rush of joy and lust each time she saw him. Her first instinct was always to run to him and kiss him, even though she wasn't normally that kind of woman.

She was in love with Kell Montrose.

"Um…Kell?" she called out.

"Yes?"

"I have a little medical emergency in the kitchen." Kell came running into the room, took one look at the bloody towel in her hand and went white. "What happened?"

"I cut myself."

"Is Mommy okay?" Sammy asked, a little tremble in his voice.

She smiled over at him where he stood in the doorway with his bare feet on the cold Spanish tile. "I'm fine."

"She will be. I'll take care of her. In case we have to go to the emergency room, why don't you go put your shoes on," Kell said. Then he came over to her, wrapped his arm around her shoulder and took the towel away from her hand and looked at the cut. "Let's rinse this off."

He put her hand under the sink and cleared the blood. As she looked down at it, she thought maybe it didn't look so bad, but blood kept flowing from the wound and she was starting to see little dots in front of her eyes. There was a roaring in her ears and she cursed as she felt everything start to go dark and she collapsed.

Twelve

Panic was Kell's first thought, but he tried to keep cool as he cradled Emma to his chest. Sammy came in and ran over to them.

"Mommy," he cried.

That's when Kell's panic cleared and he went into action.

"Get a pillow so we can lift her feet up," Kell said.

Sammy hesitated and looked down at his mom. "She'll be okay, buddy, but we need to get her feet up and then we'll see if we can find any smelling salts."

"There's salt on the table," he said. "Be right back."

Sammy ran out of the room and was back a second later. Watching the three-year-old place the pillow at Emma's feet and then carefully lift one and then the other onto it made Kell realize how hard this must be for a child who'd lost his father.

Luckily, it didn't take long before Emma opened her eyes. "Did I pass out?" she asked. "It's really not a big deal. It's just a little cut."

"Mommy. Are you okay?"

"Yes," she said, reaching for her son and hugging him to her.

She started to get up but Kell put a hand on her shoulder. "Stay there for a few more minutes."

She nodded. Her face was still pale and her lips dry and chalky. "Watch her for me, Sammy."

"I will, Darth Dada."

Kell smiled at the kid and got up to turn off the burner under the pan of sizzling chicken. Then he looked up what to do for a fainting spell on his phone. He knew that cut was pretty deep, too, and probably was going to need a stich or two.

"Do you have a first-aid kit?"

"Under the sink in the bathroom. Sammy knows where it is," Emma said.

"I'll get it," the little boy said and ran off.

Kell knelt back down beside her. "I think we need to keep pressure on your cut. I'm going to take you to the emergency room. You might need stitches."

"I'm sure it's nothing," Emma said.

"But you don't want to take any chances, so we're going," Kell said.

"Don't I get a say in this?" she asked, her eyes starting to spark with some signs of her usual personality.

He tucked a strand of hair behind her ear and smiled down at her. "No."

Sammy came back with the first-aid kit and sat down cross-legged next to his mom again, holding her hand. Kell found a bandage, which he wrapped around her finger, and then looked at Sam.

"Want me to call your aunt Cari to watch you?" Kell asked.

"Why?" Sammy asked. "You said Mommy was okay."

"She is but I have to take your mom to the doctor," Kell said.

"I want to come," Sam said.

Kell lifted Emma into his arms and then stood up a little bit awkwardly. Sammy trailed behind him, bringing the pillow as they walked to the front door. Kell got his shoes on and his keys from the table, where he'd tossed them.

"You'll have to take my car. Sammy's car seat is in it," Emma said.

"I'll get mommy's keys," Sam said. He ran up to her room and brought down her purse.

Kell didn't have time to really dwell on it but this entire situation was weird. He'd never in his life felt so out of control, so unsure of himself or what he was doing. On one hand he was glad that he'd come for dinner so he was there for Emma and could take care of her. But on the other he would have liked to have been safely at his place by himself, so he'd never have to know this much panic and fear for another person.

For two other people. Sammy was putting on a brave

front and smiling every time that Emma looked at him but when she glanced away the little boy stared at his mom with fear in his eyes. And it broke Kell's heart.

"I can stand, Kell," Emma said.

He set her on her feet but didn't want to let go of her until he was sure she was okay. Nothing had been as horrible as watching her fall on the kitchen tile earlier as she'd passed out.

"Let's go," Kell said.

He drove to a walk-in clinic because it was closer than the emergency room. Since the clinic served the local neighborhood, it wasn't busy at all. He signed Emma in as Sammy took her hand and led her over to sit down.

"Your son is doing a good job looking after his mom," the receptionist said.

Kell started to correct her, to say that Sammy wasn't his, but then realized he wanted him to be. "Yes, he is."

When he joined Sammy and his mother in the waiting area, Kell's mind was a mess, full of thoughts of the things he wanted and fears that he couldn't really be the man these two people needed. The dad Sam needed, the husband Emma needed. He even worried he wasn't the business shark he'd always been. He was losing his edge and the worst part was he didn't even mind losing it.

A nurse took Emma back to see the doctor and Sam looked over at Kell with those big brown eyes of his. The way he had the other night at the basketball game when DJ had climbed onto Dec's lap and Kell lifted Sam up and onto his lap.

Sammy wrapped one arm around Kell's shoulder. "I hope Mommy is okay."

"Me too. You've been a big help," Kell said, patting the little boy's back.

Kell took out his phone and gave it to Sammy to play with while they waited. He didn't want to be distracted by email or texts from the office. For the first time ever, his personal life was taking precedence and he was damned glad for it because he knew he loved Emma.

But he didn't truly realize it until she walked out of the back room and held up her bandaged finger. As soon as he saw her smile he knew. He felt it. Love. The one emotion he'd never thought he could feel poured into him and left no doubt as to what it was.

Idiot. That's all she could think, as she felt the ridiculous happiness of seeing Sammy and Kell waiting for her. Once again, the realization struck her. She loved Kell.

She knew that it wasn't going to be the hearts and flowers runaway love that she'd shared with Helio. But she was older now, and a much different woman. She needed more from the man she gave her heart to. And she wasn't even sure he'd want it, but that didn't change the fact that she loved him.

Kell and Sammy both stood up when they saw her. Her son ran over and hugged her tightly. She bent down and scooped him up.

"Did you have to get sewed?"

"Stitches," Emma said gently. "Yes I did. I got three."

"Just like how old I am," Sammy said.

"Exactly. Were you good for Kell?" The question was directed at Sammy but Emma looked up at Kell and he nodded at her.

"I was. We were both worried about you."

"Well, I'm fine now and we are good to go," Emma said.

Kell held the door open for them and then led the way to her car. She put Sammy in his car seat and closed the door, turning to find Kell just standing there. He didn't say anything, just drew her into his arms and held her closely, kissing the top of her head.

"I'm so glad you're okay."

"It was just a dumb cut. I should have been paying attention," she said.

"Why weren't you?" he asked.

"I was thinking about that serious conversation you wanted to have with me," she said. "Are you going to break up with me?"

He hugged her closer. "Let's go get some dinner and then after Sammy goes to bed we can talk."

"That's it, isn't it?" she asked. "Don't keep putting it off."

"I'm not, but we have a three-year-old in the car and he's hungry and worried about his mom," Kell pointed out.

"And I'm the one having a tantrum," she said at last. "I get it. I know we need to be alone to chat, but it's making me a little crazy."

"Me, too. I can't imagine ever walking away from

you, Emma, but we both know I have some less than sterling qualities."

"Okay, fair enough. We can talk later," she said. Reality could wait. She wanted a few more hours of time together where she didn't have to admit that nothing in this situation was under her control. Kell held the door for and she got into the passenger seat. A few minutes later they were on their way to a Tex-Mex cantina in the neighborhood.

They sat in a corner booth and ordered food and drinks. She wanted to just let it be an evening where from the outside they looked like a perfect family. But it was hard because she knew it wasn't true.

She was tired, and her finger was throbbing because the pain medicine the doctor had given her was wearing off. Plus, Sammy was wound up from Kell's giving him everything he asked for. Tons of sugary soda and dessert.

"Another soda?" Kell asked.

"No," Emma said. "That's enough for tonight."

"But, Mommy—"

"No buts. I'm fine now and so are you," Emma said. Then she turned to Kell. "You're spoiling him."

"I know."

She looked at him and he gave her a shrug and then looked away. Which almost made Emma feel bad that she'd said anything. But he couldn't just give Sammy the moon when he hadn't committed to being around after tonight. She almost suspected he was going overboard because he wasn't going to be here tomorrow.

And that made her feel like crying or lashing out

irrationally and yelling at him. She took a deep breath and pulled her cell phone from her purse but didn't turn it on, just stared down at the black screen for a long time trying to find her balance. But it just wasn't there.

She was a wreck. She wanted to know what was going on with Kell and she needed answers now, not in an hour or two after Sammy was asleep. She pushed the button to turn on her phone and caught her breath. She had a new home screen picture of Sammy and Kell. A selfie of them giving her the thumbs-up.

Why did Kell do things like this if he was planning to leave?

"Nice photo," she said, showing them both.

"We did it while you were in getting your finger fixed," Sammy said.

"I hope you don't mind," Kell said.

"Not at all. I like it a lot. I'm just really tired now," she said.

"You've had a long day. Let me get the check and I'll take you both home," Kell said.

He went off to settle the bill.

"I think he wants to stay with us, Mommy," Sammy said.

"Sweetie, remember what I said. He likes you and he likes me but that doesn't mean he can be your daddy."

Sammy stuck his lower lip out. All that sugar and the late hour made him a little more temperamental than usual. "I don't think that's fair."

"I'm not the one who's deciding this," she said.

"Deciding what?" Kell asked as he returned to the table. He rested his hand on the back of Sammy's chair.

Her son twisted around and looked up at Kell.

"If you can be my daddy."

Kell patted the little boy on his shoulder. "That's a big decision. I think we all need to talk before anything like that can happen."

Sammy was safely tucked into his bed and sleeping soundly when Emma came back downstairs, where she'd left Kell. He'd poured her a glass of Bailey's on the rocks and one for himself and had turned on the gas fireplace.

"This looks like romance but I think we both know that looks are deceiving."

"I'm not deceiving you at all, Emma."

"Only time will tell," she said.

Yes, it would. Tonight he'd realized that he was willing to compromise on a few things he never would have thought he would. "I guess the way I said we needed to talk was ominous and I never meant for it to come out that way."

"It was. So what's going on?" she asked, taking her glass and lifting it to her mouth for a delicate sip. She sat down next to him on the couch but left a good foot of space between them.

She curled one leg underneath her body and stared at him with that serious look that made him feel as if he could never measure up in her eyes.

"The board and I have decided that your probation has been successful. But we're going to start you out slow in your new position."

"What do you mean?"

"It'd be a position where you'd give input, but you'd need someone else to sign off on your budgets," he said.

"Are you kidding me? I mean I can see that my decisions as CEO of Infinity weren't necessarily the most sound but I was trying to stay a few steps ahead of you in your takeover bid. And you were gunning for Infinity Games," she said. "And since the takeover I haven't taken any risks."

"Except for kissing me in the elevator," he said.

"This isn't personal, or is it?" she asked. "Was that your play from the beginning?"

"You know it wasn't. But it is personal now. We can't get away from the fact that there is something between us. Something that has nothing to do with business. Listen, I've been thinking that maybe I could get the board to give you a position with a little more power in it," he said. "I will talk to them tomorrow."

"Can't you make the decision on your own?" she asked.

"I...I don't know. I'm trying to let you change me," he said, shoving his hands through his hair. God knew it was too late. She'd already changed him in ways he didn't want to let her see.

"You've changed me," she said, putting her glass down. "I know this is hard. I'm going to lay it all on the line here. I really care about you, Kell. Not just because Sammy likes you and wants you to be his new daddy but because *I* like you. I want you to stay and not for a night but for the rest of our lives.

"But that can't happen if you aren't willing to

change. We can't let doubt and generations-old hatred keep us apart. And that's what you're doing."

She made it sound so easy. Give up the hate and move on. If only. Instead, he was having a hard time believing that everything between them was real. He loved her. He'd never said those words to himself about anyone before. But he also knew that he'd never thought of having permanency before his cousins had settled down with Emma's sisters and had started raising babies.

Once again in his life, he'd felt left out. He'd been the only one without parents growing up and was the only one without a fiancée and a baby of his own now. Then he'd kissed Emma and made a place for himself in her life.

A big part of him was afraid that he'd done it just so he wasn't left out. Just so he wouldn't be alone the way he had been all his life. Tonight had tested him and stretched the boundaries of what he thought he'd wanted in his life and he'd felt fear.

The fear of knowing that now that he cared for Emma and Sam, he'd always be afraid of losing them.

"What are you thinking?" she asked. "Talk to me." She was smart and ballsy when it came to love. She went after things that he would have been afraid to.

"What if we're wrong, Emma? What if this is just about us seeing our other family members falling in love and fearing that we'll be the ones who are left all alone?" he asked.

"It's not."

"How do you know?" he asked her. "Give me something so I know this is real."

She bit her lower lip and shook her head. "I can't. I can't do what you're asking me to. Because if I took that risk…there's too much to lose."

He realized then that she didn't want to change, either. He wanted to be mad at her but really if he was unwilling to take the risk why should she?

"I guess that's the truth then. We are both too afraid to change," he said.

"Not at all. I'm afraid to say I care for you because I don't know if you're still bent on revenge."

Her words hurt and made him realize that she hadn't seen the real man. Or even worse, maybe she had. Had he become a man who'd been focused on vengeance for so long that he didn't know how to have any other kind of emotion? He simply didn't know anymore. Apparently, she still saw him as the man she'd always known. The one who had grown up in Thomas Montrose's shadow.

"Then there is nothing else to say. Because I have shown you I'm not the kind of person who'd do something like that."

She crossed her arms over her chest. "You haven't shown me that at all. I need some sign from you, Kell. Is that too much to ask?"

Thirteen

Emma wanted to take the risk—tell him she loved him and hope that the gamble paid off. But she was too afraid. The words were there in her mind and she knew all she had to do was speak them. But she couldn't.

She'd loved and lost once and though she'd thought she'd recovered enough to love again, it was now painfully obvious that she hadn't. The fault was hers and she couldn't blame him. He deserved a woman who could love him with all of who she was.

Not a woman who'd hedge her bets by letting herself get emotionally involved with a man she couldn't really commit to.

"I'm sorry."

"Me too," he said.

She walked over to him and ran her hands over the

stubble on his cheeks and then went up on tiptoe and kissed him. This time was different than every other kiss they'd shared because this time…well, this time she knew it would be the last.

Kell pulled back and looked down at her with that silvery-gray gaze of his and it was icy once again. He was back to the man she'd always known and a part of her wept deep inside but she kept her facade in place.

"I guess this is it," he said.

She'd always thought they'd end in a big fight with more passion and fire than this. But instead it felt as if two people putting down the shutters and locking themselves away. Trying to protect themselves from what was coming.

She thought of all the dinners they'd shared, the lovemaking and the laughter. And she knew that she'd never let herself believe he could stay because she didn't want him to.

"Yeah," she said.

He gathered his stuff and walked to the door as she stood there watching. Kell cursed and turned around, stalking back over to her. "Damn you, Emma. You were going to let me walk away like that, without a fight?"

"What can I do?"

"Act like this all meant something to you. I'm beginning to think you had your own plan for revenge. A very intimate sort of payback to make sure that I would suffer."

She shook her head. She knew where he was going. "I'd thought the same, but it's not true. We both were lonely…but we're loners who are used to going it alone. This isn't fair to you at all, but I can't take the risk of falling for you."

"Why not? Am I such a jerk? A loser? What is it that makes me unappealing, Emma?"

She wrapped her arms around her waist. "It's me. I'm the one who is too afraid to risk this. I just can't do it. You could die, you could change your mind, you could be playing a game with me," she said.

"Doubtful, since I just accused you of doing that. I'm willing to take the chance," he said.

"Are you really? I don't know everything about love but I know that when it's true and real it doesn't feel like fear."

"Maybe there is just too much between us to ever really trust each other," he said, quietly. He tipped his head to the side and looked over at her from under that ridiculous fall of curls on his forehead.

He looked sexy and sad and she wanted to say the hell with it, open her arms and say she'd do anything for him. He'd changed her, changed her life and made her realize things about herself that she'd thought she'd never claim again.

But another part of her knew that if he couldn't say the words she needed to hear, the little bud of love that had started to grow in her heart would wither and die. And she'd be even more broken than she had before she'd let herself care for Kell Montrose.

The man who'd been the face of the devil to her and her sisters in the last year had changed completely in her view but she was too afraid to believe those changes were real and he was too afraid to prove to her that they were. Now she was beginning to think that maybe she was projecting onto him what she desperately wanted to find.

The one thing she'd been lacking ever since she'd first walked out of the boardroom with the ultimatum ringing in her ears. She wanted what her sisters had found and she'd tried to make Kell into the man for her. It would be neat and tidy, wouldn't it?

"It's more about trusting myself. I'm trying to convince myself that it's you I really care for and not just...."

"An illusion," he said after a few moments had passed. "I'm dealing with the same doubts. I've never wanted to be part of something like this. A family. I have no idea if it's just the novelty of it or if this is the real thing. Something that could last forever."

A spark of anger went through her. "Now I'm a novelty?"

"I didn't mean it that way," he said.

"Then how did you mean it. Explain it to me. Because my son sure loves you and it has nothing to do with the novelty of having a man around."

"Really, Emma, is that how you see it? Because as far as I'm concerned, it is the rarity of having a man around who can focus his time on him that has caused Sam's attachment to me," Kell said. "Seems that as his mom you would have noticed that the one thing he really wants is a dad."

"Don't you dare criticize my mothering," she said. "I didn't bring you here to become a father to him. I was just learning to be a woman again, thinking that maybe I had a chance—you know what? That doesn't matter. All those little dreams I had were clearly wasted on you."

The words just flowed out of her and she realized they were the truth. She could have started over with any man, so why, oh, why had she chosen him?

Kell shoved his hands through his hair. Everything was going from bad to worse. All of his relationship questions seemed to be answered in this one argument. He'd known for a while that he was playing at something that wasn't real. Something that couldn't be real to him because he had absolutely no idea of how to behave in this kind of situation.

He should never have brought Sam into this. Except that the kid was just as much a reason why he wanted to figure out how to stay here with Emma and make it work. He wanted that ideal family that had been such a mirage in his childhood. A perfect shimmery image of a dad and a mom and happy kid. Maybe some siblings.

But if he was struggling to figure out how to let Emma know that he loved her, how the hell would he ever be able to let kids into his heart? He had always believed himself to be strong. A proud loner who didn't need anyone. Now he knew that he did need and want someone else in his life. And he knew that person was Emma, but he'd never be able to really admit that out loud.

He didn't want to take a chance on loving because he was comfortable alone and if he loved her and let her and Sam become a part of his life, they could be ripped away from him in a heartbeat and he'd be worse off than he was now.

"I shouldn't have said anything that sounded even remotely critical of your mothering," he said. "I'm sorry for that. And I never meant for Sammy to become attached to me. I think I understand far more than you do how much he wants a dad. It's one of the things I always craved."

"Then why are you running away?" she asked. "I know you have never had a family but I thought over the last two weeks that we'd figured out how to be one."

"We haven't. I think we've both been playing house and I want to believe that if we took a chance I'd adjust to it. But it feels like I'm pretending to be something I'm not. And you and Sam both deserve more than that."

There it was. The one truth he'd been afraid to speak and had been hoping to hide forever. The darkness inside him that made it hard for him to ever be anything other than a bitter man. The grandson of a man driven by hatred. He'd adjusted well enough to function in most situations, but this thing with Emma required more than functioning. He'd have to be real and he never had been able to.

"Fair enough. Then this really is goodbye," she said.

"Yes, it is. And you don't have to worry that this will prejudice my opinion of you at work," he said.

"I have no choice but to take your word on that. But you've been pretty fair, at least up until now," she admitted.

Once again, he was reminded of how they'd started out. Goodbye should be so easy to say to this woman. His grandfather had been swindled by hers a long time ago. Revenge had always been the name of the game. But as he stood in her hallway and felt the newfound love rise up inside him it was harder than he thought it would be. Harder to say the words that would put her forever out of reach.

But he knew he needed to ensure that she never came back to him. He knew that he had to make this break permanent because he also knew that no matter how much he wanted to believe what he felt was love, it couldn't be. He didn't believe in love. He'd seen many men do really stupid things in the name of that emotion.

Including his own cousins. And then he thought of John and Patti and how they'd thought love would give them the happily-ever-after of their dreams and had it all taken away in one quick accident. There were no guarantees, he knew this, and he'd be willing to bet that Emma knew it even more than he did.

"Business has absolutely nothing to do with any of this," he said. "I don't know why I brought it up."

"I know. We both know that you made me a promise that if I did the work—"

"I always intended to break that promise," Kell admitted. "But you've proven yourself. I meant what I said earlier. I'll go back to the board tomorrow and lobby for a position for you that entails more power. Your ideas have been instrumental in forming the new educational gaming division and you deserve to run it. This is strictly confidential, but we are currently in talks with a Japanese company to invest in Play-tone-Infinity. It may take some work bringing them on board with my decision, but I think you're the one for this job." Even though he knew the Japanese investors would frown on such an arrangement, he'd cross that bridge when he came to it. Maybe Playtone-Infinity didn't really need their investment anyway. And this was the least he could do for Emma after all they'd been through and, if he were honest, all her hard work.

"Thank you," she said softly, a look of sadness in her eyes.

"I wish I could do more. I want to be a man you can admire, one you can love, but it's hard for me to see how to make us work as a couple, Emma. I just don't believe in it or in myself. Not that way."

Emma knew that she couldn't fix Kell and knew that she herself was broken in ways she didn't want to admit. It was nice that he was trying to make it easier for her. Taking all the blame so that he was the prob-lem. She didn't stop him when he opened the door and stood there on the threshold, half in light and half in shadow.

She'd said her goodbyes with that kiss. Her fin-gers tingled from touching his stubbled jaw but her heart was heavy because once again she'd felt love slip through her fingers.

Still, she didn't do anything to stop it. She felt the cold dampness of the January air steal into her house and wrap itself around her. He was waiting, she real-ized. Just hoping she'd say something that would give him a reason to stay. And there it was again. The truth she always hid from.

She was a coward. She couldn't even take a risk to get someone she thought she wanted. So he sighed and walked out the door, closing it with a finality that echoed through her soul.

Second chances didn't come along every day. She knew that better than most, but still there wasn't a thing she could do to make herself go after him. And she had to give Kell credit for being honest. He'd admitted he had no idea how to let go of the hate of the past and really live for the present. But at least he could admit it. Something she'd been powerless to do.

She stood by her front door, looking out the window next to it, and watched as Kell stood by his car looking up at the night sky. What was he doing? Why didn't he just go?

What if he came back?

She held her breath, hoping that he would and cursing herself for a fool that she wanted him so badly but hadn't been able to speak her true feelings in the end. But it wasn't meant to be.

He got into his car and drove away. She stood there for a long time after he'd gone. Stared at the empty driveway and knew that there was a part of her heart that would always be empty, too. Just vacant. It'd be reserved for the man she loved, but she knew she'd never risk asking him to be a part of her family.

She wanted to cry but was too disappointed in herself to let the tears flow. She hadn't been betrayed by Kell the way that Cari had been by Dec or even Jessi had been by Allan. The only betrayal that Emma had experienced was by her own actions.

How sad that she had always believed that Helio's death had made her stronger and only now she knew that in reality it had left her weak. She finally had to face the fact that it had.

She moved through the empty house turning off lights and straightening up. She'd been careful to never leave any trace that Kell had spent the night so that Mrs. Hawking would catch on. Now she realized she'd been hiding him.

He'd been her guilty secret and she wondered if she'd have let it continue if she didn't have a son. Because they could have kept on seeing each other, sleeping together, both pretending that it was nothing more an affair. That it was just temporary. It was Sammy who'd driven her to the truth. He wanted a man in his life to be his daddy. But Emma had only realized that she couldn't take the chance on letting another man into her heart.

She went into the living room, picking up the cushions that Kell and Sammy had used when they'd been playing "Mario Kart." She put the controllers away and found Kell's tie lying on the floor half under the couch. She bent down to pick it up. The scent of his aftershave assailed her and she sank down on the couch cushions.

She put it to her nose and breathed deeply. She felt the warmth of tears on her cheeks. Why was she crying? She'd been the one to make the decision to let him leave. To not fight for him. To not fight for the love that she'd barely been able to admit to herself she felt.

But she knew why. She knew that no matter what lies she told to herself about being broken or about not being able to fix Kell, she had been afraid to fix herself. To do something that could make her happy because if she were wrong she'd never be able to live it down.

She hated that. Hated that she'd never realized how powerful fear could be. She'd thought that love could conquer all. Had seen it do that in her life after Helio's death when she'd held Sam in her arms for the first time and felt him wrap himself around her heart and fill in all the empty spots.

But now she knew that love couldn't banish fear. That was something she wouldn't have believed. She stayed on the couch counting her fears and trying to own them the way she had when she'd found herself widowed and pregnant.

This was worse because she knew that she had been pretending to be okay when in reality she'd never been. She'd never really loved Helio the way she loved Kell because she'd been able get over Helio eventually. And a big part of her knew that she'd never be able to get over Kell in the same way.

She had no idea what she was going to do next, but if she'd learned anything it was that life went on whether she had plans or not.

Fourteen

Kell sat in the boardroom waiting for his cousins and their fiancées to show up. He was trying hard to pretend that it was just another day at work but last night had been a hard one and he hadn't gotten any sleep. He'd realized last night at about three a.m. that he was a total idiot and he should have just admitted to loving Emma. That would have been the solution.

For a man who was known for always winning, how had he allowed himself to be defeated not by Emma or by love but by himself? He wanted the meeting to start so he could officially give her a job he knew she'd like and then talk to her. Figure out a way to win her back into his life.

He honestly believed it wouldn't be that hard. Hell, he was more than likely kidding himself with that.

But when he got out of bed this morning, sure he was very tired and frustrated about last night, but he was also hopeful that he could have the things he'd always wanted if he just trusted himself enough to reach out and take them.

"We've got problems," Dec said, walking into the boardroom and tossing a piece of paper on the table.

"Good morning to you, too," Kell said.

"It's not good. Read that and then tell me if you don't agree," Dec said.

Kell pulled the paper to him and read the news update from Gamesutra, an industry website that sent out daily updates. He skimmed the story, trying to see what had Dec so tense this morning, and then saw their names listed next to the Japanese investors they'd been talking to.

"Dammit. Who leaked this?" Kell asked. This was going to make them look weak to other companies who might think the merger had taken up more resources than it actually had. And it also made it harder for Kell to argue for what he wanted now that the entire gaming world knew what was going on.

"I have no idea. Allan and I were the only ones you talked about this with, right?" Dec asked.

Kell froze. He hadn't discussed the details but he had mentioned it to Emma. But when would she have had time to leak the information? He had to talk to her and make sure that she hadn't.

"One more person knew," Kell admitted.

"Who?" Dec demanded. "This completely undermines the work I've been putting together to take back to the investors. I mean, we look like we don't know what we are doing."

"I know," Kell said. "I'll be right back."

He walked out of the boardroom and down the hall to his office. He dialed Emma's number and she picked it up on speaker on the third ring.

"Hello, Kell."

"Emma, we need to talk before the meeting," he said. "When will you be here?"

"About ten minutes. I'm in the parking garage," she said. "I was hoping to catch you early."

"Good. Come up to my office as soon as you get into the building," he said.

"I will," she said.

He turned on his computer and starting searching for the rumors on the internet to see if he could find where they'd come from. But there was only a link to the Gamesutra article and one more vague article from another virtual gamer's blog. Kell wanted to wait before he jumped to conclusions but he felt as if this was all the evidence he needed that he'd made the right choice last night when he'd left Emma. She'd thrown him off his game.

He hadn't even read any industry emails this morning; instead he'd been moping around like some idiot in love. Thinking of ways to win her back. But now it seemed as though letting her go was the best decision he could ever have made.

He wondered again at fate or whatever it was out there that seemed to have it in for him. Was he doomed to never have a loving family of his own, aside from his cousins? His father was taken before he was old enough to know him and his mom had left and never looked back. Maybe he should just give up, considering what life always put in front of him.

He got an instant message from his assistant informing him that Emma was here and quickly messaged her back to let her in.

A moment later the door opened and Emma walked into his office. She had her large Louis Vuitton bag and her hair was pulled back in a high ponytail. She wore another tailored Chanel dress. She looked tired but smiled at him and for a minute he could only stare at her.

She was so pretty. God, it had been too long since he'd held her in his arms.

"You wanted to see me?"

"Yes, please come in and sit down. I want to show you something and then I have a few questions for you."

"Of course," she said. "When you're done I'd like to talk to you about last night."

He frowned and shook his head. "Not at the office."

"Okay. That's fine," she said, sitting down and putting her bag on the floor next to her. She crossed her legs at the ankles and looked over at him.

"Read this," he said, shoving the printout Dec had given him toward her.

She took it and he settled back in his chair to watch her reactions. He saw her slowly reading the article, watched her eyes move. And then her brow furrowed and she looked up at him.

"You think I leaked this?" she immediately asked him when she was finished.

"Did you?" he asked.

"Really? That's the kind of person you think I am?" she asked. "I can't believe this."

"Neither can I. But aside from Allan and Dec, you're the only one who knew I'd been holding discussions with them," Kell said.

She shook her head. "I've never done anything under the table or dirty in any of our negotiations even when it would have served me well to do so. You know that," she said. "That you would even think I'd do this shows me exactly the kind of man you are."

"Don't get all high and mighty. Someone had to leak it," Kell said, mad at himself and at her. Mad that instead of saying the things he wanted to say to her he was once again at odds with her.

Emma knew that he had every right to suspect her and if he'd asked her this question four weeks ago she wouldn't have a single problem with it, but he was asking her now after she'd invited him into her bed, into her body and into her heart. Granted, she hadn't been brave enough to tell him he was in her heart, but he still should have known better.

"Someone did have to leak this information," she said tightly, as she felt a tinge of disappointment and real anger roiling through her stomach, making her feel as if she might throw up.

But then being stupid about a man was enough to fill any woman with regrets. And should-have-dones.

But this felt worse, and the pain of watching him leave last night was nothing compared to this. This was betrayal of her most intimate self.

"Was it you?"

"No, Kell. I didn't leak any type of information about a potential investment from a Japanese firm. Aside from the fact that I don't know anything except that you talked to them, it's in my best interest to keep Playtone-Infinity Games on its strongest footing. I might have let you slip past my guard when you took over Infinity but I'm usually very astute when it comes to business."

He nodded. "Then who did it?"

"I don't know. I'm not in a position with any real power, remember? That's exactly how you wanted it. And you've got your wish."

She stood up and walked over to him, leaning forward and bracing her hands on his desk. "You might want to look inside your own ranks. Because as you pointed out, Allan and Dec knew and they both have staff members who report to them."

Kell leaned back.

"I will check with them both. But you were the logical choice."

"No, I wasn't," she said. "I'm a woman you've known for a long time in the business world and when has there ever been a hint of anything like this about me?"

"I haven't paid that close attention—"

"Liar. Not only that, you *know* me. We were lovers, Kell. Don't you know I wouldn't betray you?"

"Do I?"

She shook her head. "You know, last night I thought I saw something in you. Something that was broken that could be mended. That you were simply afraid to love someone because no one had ever really loved you before."

"Thanks for that," Kell said sarcastically.

"Don't thank me. Because this morning I realized that you aren't bent at all, you are completely broken, and there isn't any amount of care or love or sense of family that I can provide that can fix you."

"I don't recall asking you to fix me," he said.

"But you did when you sat on the floor and played video games with my son and when you let the receptionist at the clinic call us a family," she said. "You wanted it, or at least I thought you did. I guess you were playing one more game."

"Not at all. I don't know why you're acting like I've injured you. Questioning you about the leak was logical," he said again.

The fact that he still didn't understand why she was upset was all she needed to hear. "Don't say anything else. I get it. I didn't betray you. I never would. Even if somehow you figure out a way to fire me after today's meeting I'd still never do that."

"Why not?" he asked. "Won't you want revenge on me?"

She shook her head. If she need further proof that he could never see the world the way she did then she had it. "To what end? Should I raise Sammy to hate you and teach him everything I know about games and game-making so that one day he can go against you and his cousins and try to bring you all down?"

Kell didn't say anything but just looked up at her with that steady silver gaze. "I wouldn't blame him if he did that."

"I wouldn't either. I'd blame myself for being so shallow and weak that I couldn't see that there was more to life than being stuck in the past and always seeing the worst in every person."

She saw that her words had hit him hard. It was nothing more than she expected. He acted as if he was the big bad beast but underneath it all she'd seen that he wasn't. "Do you need anything else from me?"

He shook his head. She picked up her bag and turned and walked out of his office. She was shaking, and an inch away from letting her emotions get the better of her, but she wouldn't do that until she was home alone. She'd come here today ready to make a new start. To take on whatever role he'd decided on for her at Playtone-Infinity and make it work. Because she loved him.

And he didn't love her. Had never felt anything close to love. She supposed it was just sex to him. And she wished she'd been big enough to realize that sex was all it was. But she had to put on her damned rose-colored glasses and see love where none existed.

She tightened her grip on her bag as she entered the boardroom and put on her business smile as she saw Dec standing there.

"You're early for the meeting," he said.

Her future brother-in-law was an okay guy. He'd made some mistakes and he'd hurt her sister badly but he'd admitted it and had been willing to change. Something that Kell could never do. He'd have to admit he didn't know everything. He'd have to admit he'd been wrong when he'd spent so much time focused on revenge. He'd have to admit she meant something to him and he'd never be able to do that.

"Yes," she said.

Emma left the meeting mid-way through so the board could discuss her future. The board consisted of Kell, Allan, Dec and her sisters. But everyone agreed that Jessi and Cari couldn't be objective about Emma's future, which had led to Jessi giving them all a dirty look and warning Allan he better do what was right.

Even before the meeting started, Kell had already tracked down the leak to someone on Allan's staff who'd been disgruntled about the original merger with Infinity Games. Kell knew immediately that he needed to apologize to Emma but she wouldn't meet his eyes during the discussion of her new role and her body language had made it clear she wasn't going to stay behind and talk to him.

He wanted to follow her out of the boardroom but he had to have a discussion with his cousins.

"We all know Emma's ideas are solid," Dec said. "I'm in favor of making her the head of the new educational division, now that we've decided to make it a for-profit enterprise."

"I agree," Allan said. "She's smart and has proven she can lead a division and until we started our maneuvering she was doing well leading Infinity. We have the headcount for an executive. I can go over the financials one more time just to make sure we're still solid, but I don't think it will be a problem."

"Good. I'll make the official offer to her as soon as I hear back from you. Today would be best," Kell said. He had a feeling that Emma was going to run out of his life and he was never going to be able to get her back.

"Dec, it was a member of Allan's staff who leaked information about our visit from the Japanese. He's already been terminated and escorted off the property. That's why I was late to the meeting," Kell said.

"I'm glad we found the leak," Dec said. "And I know we've sort of discussed this but I don't think we should be taking on investors at this time. Their offer was flattering but I want a chance to keep this a family-run games company. There aren't many of them left."

"Me, too," Allan said. "We have the next generation to think of, wouldn't you agree?"

Kell suspected his cousins knew he'd been dating Emma. There was no other way to construe the time he'd spent at her house and he knew Sammy talked to little DJ when they were together. "I agree."

"You owe me twenty bucks," Dec said to Allan.

"Why?"

"I told him you and Emma were getting together," Dec said.

"What? Why would you think that?"

"Because you've been having dinner at her house. Sammy's sweet but he's a little gossip when bribed with chocolate," Dec said.

"Well, you're wrong. We tried it but it didn't work out."

"How did that happen?" Allan asked. "She's so much nicer than Jessi, and those Chandler girls are easy to love."

"They are," Dec said. "What happened?"

"I'm not," Kell said.

"Not what?"

"Easy to love," Kell said. He wasn't going to discuss this any further. He started gathering his iPad and his notes from the meeting and stood up.

"Wait a minute," Allan said. "What do you mean?"

Kell shook his head. "I'm not talking about it."

"Too bad. Tell us what happened?"

Kell didn't know how to explain it without sounding like…like himself. Not the persona he put on for everyone to see but the parts of himself that he didn't like and usually kept hidden away.

"Crap. You accused her of being the leak, didn't you?" Dec asked. "Damn. That's my fault. I should have done some research before just throwing it at you."

"It's cool, Dec. I did ask her about it. It was logical," Kell pointed out. "You both know that. In the business world that's how things work."

Allan gave a cynical laugh. "Jessi would have kicked my ass if I'd asked her about being the leak. Women are different. Surely, you have figured that out."

"Yes. But I would have to be someone I'm not," Kell said.

Dec nodded. "I get it. It's hard to trust. Believe me, after growing up the way we did it's very hard."

He was surprised that Dec had put what he was feeling so eloquently. But his cousin knew what he was talking about—he'd been adopted and had never really felt accepted as a Montrose, even though both Kell and Allan considered him closer than a blood relative.

"I don't know what to do. I'd have to admit…."

"That you love her," Dec said. "Hardest words to say. Ever."

"Why is that? And why doesn't she just understand how I feel?" Kell asked.

"Because you've got her messed up, too," Allan said. "That's how it was for Jessi and me. We both knew we had something there but neither of us wanted to be the first one to admit it."

Kell could see that with Allan and Jessi since they'd spent most of their adult lives as adversaries, but it was different with Emma and him. She'd been in love before. It should have been easier for her to reach out to him.

He slammed his head on the table as he remembered the shy smile she'd had on her face in his office. That she'd wanted to discuss something personal with him and he'd been too focused on accusing her of betraying him. She had been ready to reach out to him.

And he'd reacted the way he always did. "I'm a Montrose through and through."

"What do you mean?" Dec asked.

"I'm really good at killing off anything that seems

like it might be close to love. It's my one true skill. You should both be glad you aren't like me."

Allan punched him in the arm. "We are like you. You're a guy and the way you're acting right now tells me that you do love Emma."

"Of course, I do. That's never been a question in my mind," Kell said.

"Then what is?" Dec asked.

"If I can really be a part of her family," Kell said. "I don't know how to live with people I care about."

"Given how you've kept the three of us together, I'd have said that's bull. Maybe it's time you forgot the past and the way that Grandfather used us and ask Emma for forgiveness and to be your wife."

Fifteen

Here it was, two weeks after Kell and she had broken up and she was still trying to get over him. She'd taken the job they'd offered her as executive vice president of educational games, but then had asked for a two-week vacation, which had been approved. She'd taken Sammy and gone to Madrid, where Helio's family had spoiled them both.

She'd finally been able to see that she wasn't really afraid of letting herself love again. Because she was surrounded by people who loved her. Her sisters, her son and her deceased husband's family. Her main problem was trusting Kell, and she knew she could have been a little easier on him but at the same time he should never have jumped to the conclusion that she'd betrayed him. And having done so, he should have apologized.

She took a deep breath and tipped her head back to look up at the February sun shining down on her. It was Valentine's Day, and it would be so easy to blame the love-focused holiday on her current blues. But she had a feeling it was more a broken heart.

She had another few minutes before she had to be back in her office. For a moment, she'd had to escape all the flower deliveries and talk of romantic dinners from her team. But they were all wonderful people and she already loved her new role. At least she was grateful to Kell for that.

"Mommy?"

"Sammy?" she asked, turning to see her son standing next to the bench she was sitting on outside the building. "What are you doing out here? Are you okay?"

"Yes, I am. Miss Daisy brought me out here."

Emma scooped her son up for a quick hug as she noticed his day care teacher standing by the door. She waved at Emma and Emma waved back.

"Did you need me?" she asked, settling him on her lap. He had his tablet in his hands.

"Yes. I wanted to show you something."

"What is it?" she asked, smoothing his hair and kissing the top of his head. He'd stopped asking about Kell being his daddy but they'd had a long talk about how sometimes adults didn't get along. She doubted he'd understood it but when she started crying in Madrid the last time he asked, he'd stopped.

"This," he said, sliding his finger across the screen and opening up the video player. "Use these."

He pulled a pair of headphones from his pocket and gave them to her. She popped them in her ears and then re-settled Sammy on her lap. "I'm ready."

He pushed Play and the video began showing Sammy playing his piano on the tablet. Then her son looked up at the camera and started singing "They Can't Take That Away From Me."

"This is sweet, honey," she said to him.

"Keep watching, Mommy."

A few seconds further in she heard the sound of a trumpet and saw Kell move into picture. He was playing the virtual trumpet on another tablet. Then at the point at the song when Louis Armstrong usually started singing, Kell started to sing.

He stared straight into the camera and sang to her. And she felt her heart beat a little faster. She listened to the song all the way to the end and then as the music ended, Sammy and Kell looked straight at the camera and said, "No one can take the three of us from each other."

She took the ear buds from her ears. She didn't know what to say.

"What did you think?" Kell asked from behind her. She turned in her seat to look over at him.

"I loved it," she said. "I'm not sure—"

"Sammy, will you go with Miss Daisy and let us talk for a few minutes?" Kell asked.

"Yes. I'm glad you liked the video, Mommy,"

Sammy said, scooting off her lap and then running back to his teacher.

Kell stood there next to the bench and he looked good. He was clean-shaven and had on a pair of dark sunglasses. His thick curly hair was still rakishly draped over his forehead and as he sat down next to her she noticed he wore the same spicy aftershave.

"I hope you don't mind that I borrowed your song and sang it with Sammy," Kell said.

"Not at all. I am a little confused as to why," she said. "The last we talked—"

"I acted like an ass. I'm not saying I wasn't justified to ask you if you knew where the leak came from, but I should have trusted you," he said. "I'm sorry."

"It's okay. I sort of get it. Besides we'd already decided we couldn't make a relationship work." She wasn't quite sure what he was after here but she wasn't going to allow herself to jump to any conclusions.

"No, we didn't. I was waiting for you to tell me how you felt and make it so I wouldn't have to admit what I have known for a while now."

"What's that?" she asked.

"That I love you. That I like the man I am when we're together and if you'll give me a second chance I'd like to try really having a relationship with you," he said.

"I love you too, Kell. But I don't know if love is enough," she said.

"That's why I want us to take it slow and see where things go. I want a chance to be a part of your family.

Really a part of it as a stepdad to Sammy and a husband to you. Will you give me a chance?" he asked.

She hesitated. He was offering her everything that she wanted but she had to admit she was afraid to take it. What if she said yes and it didn't work out?

"I'm scared," she admitted. "I love you, Kell."

"Then don't be scared. Together we are strong enough to face anything."

She nodded. "You think so?"

She was hesitating and she knew why. She didn't want to give in to the fact that he loved her just in case he changed his mind.

"I know so."

He pulled her into his arms and kissed her. He pulled back to whisper in her ear, "I don't have a future without you by my side."

"Me either," she said.

Two months later Kell was ready to admit that he'd let go of the past. They'd fully merged Infinity Games into Playtone and Emma's education division was off to a running start. He had the one thing he'd always wanted—some peace from the bitterness his grandfather had raised him with.

He had adjusted easily to domesticated life and sometimes Emma said that was because he'd always wanted to be a part of a family. There was a time when that woman was too smart for her own good.

His cousins and Emma's sisters were coming over to her house today for a barbecue and he was planning to formally ask Emma to marry him. He'd had the ring since Valentine's Day, but it hadn't felt right to ask her then. He'd needed a little bit of time to let them both feel confident that they were together for the right reasons.

They'd had a few bumps but only because Kell couldn't say no to anything Sammy asked for. Kell knew it was because he'd always wanted someone to spoil, but Emma put her foot down and told him that both she and Sammy would still love him even if he didn't give them the moon.

"I brought the sparkling wine," Dec said, coming out onto the patio.

"Thanks."

"Wouldn't beer have been better?" Dec asked. "It's kind of the beverage for grilled food."

"Not today. Besides, I have plenty in the little fridge. Pop the sparkling wine in there and grab us both a Corona."

Cari came over to give Dec a hug and DJ and Sammy were racing around the patio with the remote controlled cars that Kell had purchased for him. As always, he was impressed by how good Sammy was with his little cousin, the way he took the other boy under his wing and showed him how to do things.

"Can you keep your sister in the house until Allan and Jessi get here?" Kell asked Cari.

"I can. Why?"

"I need to get something set up out here."

"Okay. Do you know what's going on?" she asked Dec.

"Nope," he said, kissing his wife as she went back inside.

"So?"

"I just want everything perfect before Emma comes out here," Kell said, starting to feel nervous. What if this was a mistake and she said no. He should have just asked her in bed this morning before everyone came over.

But then he knew that he wasn't going to let fear rule him. That he had almost lost her before because of that fear. He wasn't going to do that again.

"Help me hang this up," he said to Dec.

Allan came out on the patio carrying little Hannah. She smiled and squirmed in her father's arms until he put her down. She crawled over to her cousins, and seeing the three children together, Kell had a sense of rightness come over him.

It was too bad his grandfather had held on to his hatred for so long instead of bringing his family together like this. He and his cousins could have had a much better life.

But he wasn't complaining. They were all happy now and that was what mattered.

"What's up?" Allan asked. "Cari said 'boys only' outside."

"I'm going to ask Emma to marry me and needed to get everything set up," Kell said.

"Great. We were wondering when you were going to get around to it," Allan said. "Jessi is planning to corner you today."

"Just what I need," he said. "Sammy, you ready?"

"Yes, I am," Sammy said, coming over with his little car. He put the ring box in the top of the convertible.

"Once your mom comes out and I go down on my knees, send the car over, okay?"

"I will," Sammy said. "Then you can really be my daddy, right?"

"Yes."

"What's going on out here?" Emma asked, stepping out onto the patio.

"We have something to ask you," Sammy said.

"You do? I hope it's not about the go-kart again. I already said no," Emma reminded him.

"It's not," Sammy said. "Darth Dada?"

Even though Kell wasn't a big fan of it, the name had grown on him. He heard Jessi snickering behind Emma and shook his head at her.

"Emma, I hope these last few months have proven to you how much I love you."

She smiled at him and gave him a kiss. "They certainly have."

"For me too," he said. "I think you know that I'm committed to you but it's time I made it official. Will you marry me?"

He got down on one knee and Sammy, who was still standing next to him, just took the box from the car and handed it to Kell.

He opened it and looked up at Emma Chandler— once his enemy and now his future. She nodded and then said, "Yes!"

He put the ring on her finger and got to his feet to kiss her properly and thoroughly. And then they were surrounded by their family, who congratulated them. And he knew that he'd finally put the ghosts of the past to rest and found the family he'd always craved.

* * * * *

If you loved this Baby Business story,
don't miss the rest of the series,

HIS INSTANT HEIR
BOUND BY A CHILD

Available now from USA TODAY
bestselling author Katherine Garbera
and Harlequin Desire!

Still can't get enough of Kathy? Then check out her
Harlequin Blaze miniseries Holiday Heat, debuting
in November 2014,

IN TOO CLOSE
UNDER THE MISTLETOE
AFTER MIDNIGHT

Wherever Harlequin books are sold.

What if Matthew Beaumont could look at her without
caring about who she'd been in the past?

What if—what if he wasn't involved with anyone?

Whitney didn't hook up. That part of her life was dead
and buried. But…a little Christmas romance between the
maid of honor and the best man wouldn't be such a bad
thing, would it? It could be fun.

She hurried to the bathroom, daring to hope that
Matthew was single. He was coming to dinner tonight
and it sounded as if he would be involved with a lot of the
wedding activities.

Although…it had been a long time since she'd attempted
anything involving the opposite sex. Making a pass at the
best man might not be the smartest thing she could do.

Even so, Whitney went with the red cashmere sweater—
the kind a single, handsome man might accidentally brush
with his fingers—and headed out. The house had hallways
in all directions, and she was relieved when she heard
voices—Jo's and Phillip's and another voice, deep and
strong. Matthew.

She hurried down the steps, then remembered she was trying to make a good impression. She slowed too quickly and stumbled. Hard. She braced for the impact.

It didn't come. Instead of hitting the floor, she fell into a pair of strong arms and against a firm, warm chest.

Whitney looked up into a pair of eyes that were deep blue. He smiled down at her and she didn't feel as if she was going to forget her own name. She felt as if she'd never forget this moment.

"I've got you."

He did have her. His arms were around her waist and he was lifting her up. She felt secure.

The feeling was *wonderful*.

Then, without warning, everything changed. His warm smile froze as his eyes went hard. The strong arms became iron bars around her and the next thing she knew, she was being pushed not up, but away.

Matthew Beaumont set her back on her feet and stepped clear of her. With a glare that could only be described as ferocious, he turned to Phillip and Jo.

"What," he said, "is Whitney Wildz doing here?"

Don't miss
A BEAUMONT CHRISTMAS WEDDING
By Sarah M. Anderson

Available November 2014 from Harlequin® Desire.

HARLEQUIN®

Desire

POWERFUL HEROES... SCANDALOUS SECRETS... BURNING DESIRES!

**Explore the new tantalizing story from
the *Texas Cattleman's Club: After the Storm* series**

SHELTERED BY THE MILLIONAIRE

**by *USA TODAY* bestselling author
Catherine Mann**

As a Texas town rebuilds, love heals all wounds....

Texas tycoon Drew Farrell has always been a thorn in
Beth Andrews's side, especially when he puts the kibosh
on her animal shelter. But when he saves her daughter
during the worst tornado in recent memory, Beth sees
beneath his prickly exterior to the hero underneath.
Soon, the storm's recovery makes bedfellows of these
opposites. Until Beth's old reflexes kick in—should she
brace for betrayal or say yes to Drew once and for all?

Available ***NOVEMBER 2014***
wherever books and ebooks are sold.

Talk to us online!
www.Facebook.com/HarlequinBooks
www.Pinterest.com/HarlequinBooks
www.Twitter.com/HarlequinBooks

HD733491